SWEET CHRIST

Stuck WITH MY Christmas Crush

FRANCESCA SPENCER

Copyright © 2024 by Francesca Spencer

All rights reserved.

No portion of this book may be reproduced in any form without written permission from the publisher or author, except as permitted by U.S. copyright law.

Stuck With My Christmas Crush is dedicated to the fabulous team who tirelessly and gleefully made this series fly.

I love you. End of.

Chapter 1

Jason

"Come on, Maddie. We don't want to keep your mom waiting." I open the car door and stand aside as my niece climbs into the back seat of my Chevy. "Remember to buckle up."

"Of course, Jason. You treat me like a child."

"You're six years old, Maddie. You qualify."

She huffs at me as I check her seatbelt and then carefully shut the door.

"Rocko." My dog, a mastiff cross, lifts his floppy ears and tilts his head. He listens, alert and attentive. "Be on guard til I get back, okay?" I check the time on my Fitbit. "Between fourteen-thirty and fifteen hundred hours."

"He really understands, doesn't he?" says Maddie, more of a statement than a question, as I get into the driver's seat and start the engine.

"Yup. He's a very smart dog." I turn around to face Maddie. "All set? You got everything?"

"I think so."

"Let's go."

I shift the truck into gear and drive slowly through the open gate. The engine chugs as I slip into neutral, pull on the handbrake and get out to shut the gate behind me. I pull the hefty chain through the impressive wrought iron gates, but I don't bother securing the padlock. From the road, the gates look shut and locked, and with Rocko on patrol, there's little chance of an intruder chancing his luck.

"Good boy." My dog sits patiently behind the gate as I get back into my truck. I watch him in the rearview as I make a final adjustment to the mirror. His eyes don't lose focus as I drive to the road. He's still in the same spot when I make the turn in the direction of the main highway.

"Did you have fun today?" I flick a glance at Maddie who is looking out of the window. She's bundled up in her cute pink woolly hat and padded jacket.

"Yes, Jason. Thanks for asking. Rocko and I had a lovely time."

"That's good. I'm glad. It's always a pleasure to have your company, Maddie."

My niece has started talking in a way that she thinks sounds like a princess since I moved into the Mansion Hotel. Maddie loves the ramshackle, dilapidated, moldering pile. Me, not so much.

I'm only there for a short time, living in the tiny gatehouse on the once-grand estate. The situation is not ideal. And, to be honest, inheriting a property like this one is a massive headache. But, I signed the papers and now I'm the proud owner of a serious money pit. Bills started rolling in even before the ink dried at the lawyer's office, making my head spin, my bank account set to freefall, and my stomach tie itself in anxiety knots. Conveniently, I'm in between contracts at the present time. I told my agent to hold off putting me forward for anything until after the holidays. So, here I am, overseeing the inventory and imminent sale of the land, buildings, and chattels therein. I can't wait to flick it off and move on to my next engineering job, wherever that may be. Until such times, and because there needs to be someone onsite for security reasons, it just seemed obvious that I would move in. Temporarily. Just until things get sorted out, or until I get some kind of security system installed. I want to be free of this burden and get my life back. The sooner the better.

"Can you play some Christmas music?"

"Really?"

"Yes. We can sing along."

"Maddie. I'd really rather not."

"Jason. Don't be such a Grinch."

"I'm not a Grinch. I just don't want jingle bells when I'm driving... It's distracting."

"Fine. But, you know, you're heading for the naughty list, and you won't get any presents."

Maddie sees me looking at her in the rearview and huffs. She looks out of the window again, her hands clasped in her lap like the portrait of the lady in the Mansion Hotel's grand entrance hall.

My niece is adorable, although demanding. She melts my heart, and I love my role as uncle, although Maddie just calls me Jason, without the label.

"Look, Jason. There's a fairy driving a ladybug," says Maddie as I drive past a red VW at the side of the road which has been painted with black dots. The car is stationary. Its hazard lights are on. "Hey. I think it's the same fairy who came to Isabel's party."

"Maddie. Do you think there might be more than one fairy?" I can't believe what I just said. I laugh to myself, bite my lip, and roll my eyes.

"Well, duh. Of course, there's more than one fairy. I can name them for you, if you want."

"No, that's okay." I slow down and indicate a U-turn. "The fairy looks like she needs some help. Let's go ask?"

"Sure."

The road from the mansion links up to the main highway north and south, but it's windy and narrow and, unless you live up here, there's no advantage to using this route. The lack of traffic means that the road is not well-maintained and takes you up and over a hill instead of around it. I hardly ever see another vehicle when I'm driving to or from Ridgewood, the nearest town, about an hour away.

As I approach the ladybug car, the fairy lowers her phone and pulls the light-colored faux fur jacket tightly around her shoulders. She eyes me suspiciously as I park the Chevy close by in front of her.

"Hey there," I say, getting out and beginning to walk toward the young woman all decked out in glittery pink. "We noticed your hazards are on. Is everything alright?"

"Hi there. Thanks for stopping. Bertie's broken down. But I called the roadside assistance." The fairy holds up her phone as if showing me proof of her actions. "They should be here soon," she says with a nervous smile.

"It might be something simple like a dead battery," I offer. "Do you have jumper cables? I have some in the truck." I turn to point over my shoulder, then notice Maddie is at my side.

"Excuse me, fairy," says Maddie in her most polite princess voice. "Were you at my friend, Isabel's party in the summertime?"

The fairy seems to relax at the sight of a little girl and gets out of her car.

"Isabel. Mmmm. Let me see." The fairy considers Maddie's question. "Was that the party at a big white house? Does your friend have a naughty cat called Custard who tried to jump onto the table to eat the cake?"

"That's right!" says Maddie, delighted. She turns to me and beams a bright smile. "It is her. See, I told you."

"Maddie is seldom wrong." I reach out to stroke Maddie's hair. She leans casually onto my leg.

"Don't you remember?" Maddie says, looking up at me.

I glance from Maddie to the glittery girl and see something familiar in her eyes. A fleeting memory flashes of the warm summer's day when I picked Maddie up from her friend's party. As I arrived on the street outside Maddie's friend's house, a van pulled away and, for a second, I was caught in the gaze of an incredibly pretty woman; the same pretty woman who is standing beside the broken red, black-spotted, ladybug car.

"No. Sorry Maddie, I don't," I lie, but the fairy looks at me and recognition lights up her face.

She's about to say something. Her pretty lips open, then, in an instant, she checks herself, and they close again. A hand covers her mouth.

I'm conscious that I may be staring but I'm mesmerized by her face which is decorated with swirls and daubs of glittery paint. Her clear blue eyes sparkle more than the sequins on her dress.

To distract myself, I clear my throat with a cough then say, "So, do you want to get a jumpstart? Or maybe you might be out of gas, in which case, I can tow you to a gas station?"

"That's kind of you, sir," the fairy says looking directly into my eyes. "But don't let me hold you up. A trained professional is on their way." The fairy checks her phone. "They'll be here in a few minutes. At least, that's what the guy said." She laughs. "Thanks anyway."

"If you are sure you're okay," I say as Maddie reaches up and takes my hand. "Then, we'll be off."

"No," says Maddie emphatically stamping her foot. "We can't leave her here."

"Don't worry Maddie." The fairy crouches down, smiles at my niece, and whispers, "I have special magic, so I'll be okay."

Maddie thinks for a moment, then says, "If you have special magic, then you should use it to fix your car."

"Good point. And I would if I could but sadly, my poor car, Bertie, has been cursed by an evil wizard, and the only way the curse can be lifted is by a roadside assistance technician wizard." The fairy stands up and pats the hood of the little VW. Then she looks at me and says, "I'm fine. Really. But thanks, again, for stopping." She turns to climb into her car but pauses to wave and says, "Bye Maddie. Say hi to Isabel and Custard when you see them again, okay?"

"Okay, I will," Maddie says back. "Nice to see you again fairy Charlie."

"Charlie?"

"Yup. Fairy Charlie. That's me." The fairy smiles and, pulling the jacket tighter around her, she says, "And Merry Christmas."

"Alright." I stand still for an awkward moment, glancing up and then down, the road as I decide what to do. "We should get going. Maddie go get in the car. And make sure you..." Maddie finishes my sentence.

"Buckle up. I know."

Part of me wants to stay until the roadside recovery people arrive, but I promised Meredith that Maddie would be home by now. I check my Fitbit. I'll need to call my sister to say we're going to be late. I'm about to offer Charlie a ride to wherever she needs to be, but her phone rings.

"I'd better get this," she says, stepping into her car. "Thanks again." She closes the door and waves at me through the windshield.

Reluctantly, I drive away.

Chapter 2

Charlie

I regret my decision to take Belleview Road, to avoid the snarl-up on the main highway, almost immediately, as a loud clunk from somewhere underneath Bertie is followed by an ominous whirring sound. Then, there's no power as my foot pumps the accelerator and I coast over to the side of the road. And stop.

Part of me is thankful that this broken car drama didn't happen while I was on the four-lane highway. But as I take in the empty road, up ahead and behind, this situation sucks every which way I look at it.

I find my phone and call Lou to tell her what's happened. Her phone clicks straight to voicemail, so I leave a message in my best calm, I-can-handle-this voice.

"Hey Lou... So, it's all on me if I get hacked to pieces, huh? Taking an alternative route to avoid traffic and then this happens. Alright. So maybe I shouldn't have said the ax-murder bit out loud. Haha. I hope you guys got home safe. I'm going to call roadside assistance now. Love you. See you very soon. Muah!"

I hang up the call and take a moment to breathe and assess my predicament. Bertie's engine trouble might be something as simple as a busted fan belt. Do cars even have fan belts these days? I remember an old black and white film where the very glamorous heroine fixed her broken down car by removing her pantyhose, tying the elasticated length into a loop, thus stylishly replacing the busted fan belt without chipping a nail, removing her headscarf, or wayfarers. I pop the hood in preparation to investigate, although I have no idea what I'm investigating.

Maybe Bertie stopped because he's out of gas? Unlikely, as I filled up this morning. Unless someone siphoned it out while we were performing at the event. I've seen that somewhere too, although I can't remember where. Also,

I know what happens when Bertie is out of gas. It has happened before, and it was nothing like this. When Bertie ran out of gas, he just stopped. There wasn't the clunk or the whirring. I suddenly feel a bit overwhelmed by being broken down at the side of a very quiet country road. But I'm determined to remain positive and not to give in to despair or my over-active theatrical imaginings.

As if holding my phone is keeping me calm, I scroll through my contacts and find the roadside assistance number. I hit dial and wait. The ringtones fade in and out which isn't a good sign regarding connectivity, but at last, someone on the other end of the line picks up.

"Road Recovery. How may I help you today?"

The friendly operator takes my details and tells me that there's a three-hour wait for a recovery vehicle to come and assist. She asks if that would be okay. I say, not really, but what choices do I have? Then, she says that I should stay with the vehicle and have my phone switched on to receive calls from the recovery vehicle driver.

"That's all fine and dandy," I say trying to sound upbeat and positive but knowing I probably don't because my phone is almost out of charge. "It was charging in the car but now the car is non-functional, so that's not happening anymore." I check the screen to see I have two bars remaining.

"We're doing what we can ma'am and we'll be with you as soon as possible."

The operator hangs up as a late-model dark blue Chevrolet pickup passes me, heading in the direction of Ridgewood. It must have come out of a driveway because it definitely wasn't on the road behind me. The Chevy stops and makes a U-turn. I hold my phone poised to dial the police, hoping the two bars of charge will be enough to make an emergency call. The Chevy stops in front of Bertie. My heart is pounding in my throat when the driver's door opens and a tall, well-built guy gets out. He walks towards me. I'm frozen in my seat, but then I pull myself together. Shoulders back. Chin up.

The handsome driver asks if I'm okay and if I need any help. I'm still untrusting but then a little girl hops down from the backseat and asks me if I was the fairy at her friend's party.

How cool that she remembers. It takes me a while to think back to a birthday party for a little girl called Isabel. She was six years old and her cat, Custard, caused a commotion because he jumped on the food table to eat the carrot cake. I think he was just interested in licking the cream cheese frosting, and not eating the cake. I'm pretty sure cats don't like carrots.

Thinking about Custard and the carrot cake commotion suddenly jolts my memory, and I recognize the handsome Chevy driver. I thought he looked familiar, but my current headspace had attached his features to a police identikit image of a serial killer, and not the hot guy who turned up at a little girl's summer birthday party as I was leaving. I'm trying not to stare. He didn't have a beard then, and he wasn't wearing a roll-neck sweater and puffer jacket. I only caught a glimpse through the van window as Lou was driving away, but I remember him, for sure.

There are some things that are so rare and beautiful - such as a four-leaf clover; or a pink sapphire; or the Northern Lights; or a unicorn; or a hot guy at a kid's birthday party – that you just don't forget.

Lou, who was also performing at that party, spotted him too as she pulled away from the curb.

"Gosh, what a nice-looking man," she said with obvious appreciation.

"Where?"

"Honestly, Charlie. You're a terrible liar." Lou steers the van into the traffic. "I saw you looking."

"Louise. It's a fact." I say adamantly. "There are no sexy guys at kids' birthday parties. And, if there were, we shouldn't be looking. It's not right."

"No, my friend. It is not a fact. There are sexy guys. But they are, mostly, all taken." Lou leans an elbow across to nudge me. "But you are allowed to look. That is a fact."

"No, Lou. I am a highly trained professional performer, and I don't notice such banal things. Checking out hot guys is beneath me. I don't stoop to such base levels, especially when I'm wearing fairy wings and glitter."

We drive on in silence for a moment, then Lou says, "Acknowledging the beauty of a person, male or female, is like admiring a painting, or a piece of art. You can appreciate the pleasing aesthetic..." She glances at me and smiles. "...from a distance."

Louise knows me too well. I try not to notice 'pleasing aesthetic' in a man because the last time I did, it was disastrous. I ended up an emotional wreck from a relationship that was taxing from the start, to a breakup that was messy and awful, at the end. I never want to go through that kind of pain and heartache ever again.

Luckily, my wonderful friend and her partner, Calvin, had a spare room at their place for me to escape to. And hugs and a fridge full of food. It's a temporary address that I still reside at two years down the track. I am so grateful for their love and care.

Still, my roommate status is only until I get things figured out. But every time I raise the subject of moving on,

Lou shakes her head and says, "Why? We love having you here." She tells me my contribution in rent helps pay the mortgage. So, I'm still in their spare room. And happily so. For now.

I pull my faux fur jacket up around my shoulders as my mind reflects on that sunny August afternoon. As Lou and I drove away, I said, "Well done," out loud. Like Phoebe in the episode of *Friends* with Brad Pitt, when she sends up a prayer to the heavens acknowledging the creation of a truly excellent male human. Yes. Well done on creating a gorgeous man, however out of reach.

So, from a safe distance, I hold the memory of the hot guy from the summer birthday party like a secret treasure I can take out and look at any time I want. Like a beautiful picture on a gallery wall - his handsome face; his broad shoulders; his dark, wavy hair; the light in his eyes when they met mine through the van window. Pow! The image is crystalized in a freeze-frame that I can replay over and over in my mind. No one else needs to know.

Standing beside my broken beetle, at the side of the road, the vivid realization slowly dawns like a fuzzy image through a viewfinder coming into sharp focus. My eyes widen, and I close my mouth because the hot guy from the summer party is the same hot guy standing in front of me now. The drumming in my chest is for a different reason than hopeless despair.

Although, the handsome man on the roadside in front of me could still be a savage serial killer, after weighing up the facts and evidence – the little girl and the kind offer of a jump start - the probability might be illustrated with a diagonal down-sliding graph, where the point of absolutely positive one-hundred-percent chance of death and mutilation is high up on the y axis, and descends to a point on the x axis, at an absolute zero chance of death and mutilation.

My hand covers my mouth and a wave of relief washes over me. I almost faint.

The little girl is concerned about leaving me at the side of the road, but I convince them that I'm fine and help is on the way.

"Merry Christmas," I say as I wave goodbye.

Maddie gets back into the cab, but the hot guy stays. We stand facing each other, caught in a moment where neither of us moves along. He seems hesitant to leave. Then my phone rings, which breaks the moment. It's the roadside recovery people.

"I'd better get this," I say with my best bravest smile. The hot guy smiles, nods, then turns to leave.

Chapter 3

Jason

"Hey, Mom." Maddie jumps down from the back of the Chevy in my sister's driveway.

"Hey, sweetie. How was your morning at the mansion? Were you good and helpful?"

"Yes. Yes, I was. Wasn't I, Jason?"

"So good and so helpful." Meredith picks up Maddie and cuddles her.

"Thanks so much for taking her this morning. I'm all caught up now."

"No problem. I love my time with Maddie. And I have to make the most of it now, before she becomes an obnoxious teenager in a couple of years."

"I'm never going to be an obnoxious teenager, whatever that is," says Maddie emphatically.

"Do you want to stay for dinner?"

"No. I'm going to get back and keep sorting stuff out. But it is endless. There are so many boxes and trunks. Every wardrobe seems to be full of junk. Really. I just want to torch the place."

"I don't think you are approaching this with the right frame of mind, soldier." Meredith lowers Maddie to the ground. She runs off inside the house. "You have been left a sizable property by a distant relative we didn't even know existed. Don't you want to find out about her, and the people who owned the place? Their story? I mean, it was a hotel and quite expensive and fashionable in its day. There could be all sorts of treasures hidden in the walls and attic. I think it's exciting."

"It might be for you. You're not there and dealing with it." I grit my teeth and run my hand through my hair with exasperation. "I just want to get rid of the place so I can move along. At the moment, it's actually costing me to be there. And the longer I hang on to it, the greater the expense which means the less we'll get when it does sell." I pause then change my tone. "Don't you want your share?"

"Yes. It would be a welcome bonus for sure. We're probably going to set up a trust fund or something for Maddie. But Daniel and I have good jobs." Meredith smiles kindly, her head drops slightly to one side. "I fully appreciate you taking responsibility for selling the property. And, selfishly, I kind of like my brother living within uncle-duty distance. For a while. It's great having you nearby after all the time you've been away. I know Maddie likes it."

"Yeah. I should focus on the upside. It is good to be living a short drive away from my favorite sister."

"Your only sister." Meredith play-punches my arm.

I laugh and pull my car keys out of my pocket. "And it's ex-soldier, by the way."

"I know, Jason. But part of you is always going to be in Afghanistan." Meredith can see right through me. I've left the military, but the military hasn't left me. "You can get a contract anytime." She shrugs. "But inheriting the mansion is an unexpected gift. Have some grace about that."

"You're right, Meredith." I laugh again. "I've contacted the real estate agent, to get things rolling." I shake my head and sigh at the endless list of things that need to be done to get the house ready for sale. And I think about all the things I'd rather be doing instead of packing up a big old empty house.

"I'll come and give you a hand next week, alright."

"Thanks."

"It must be lonely out there. On your own."

"I'm not really on my own. I have Rocko. He's great company. Anyway, it's Christmas soon and nothing is set to move in the property market until the entire legal profession sobers up after New Year, so there's no real rush. Looks like I'm stuck there for a few weeks at least."

"Well, try and find the joy in it. Otherwise, it'll be a drag and you get so boring when you're grumpy. No one wants that. Not me or Maddie. Got it?"

"Got it. Look on the bright side," I say as if articulating the words will affect my negative mindset.

"There you go." Meredith punches me again on the other arm this time. "And about Christmas. Are you going to grace us with your presence and presents this year?"

"Oh, I don't know. It's nice to be invited and... It's just not..."

"Maddie will be disappointed if you're not here with us."

"I'll need to sort out some security up at the mansion and there's Rocko to consider... Any other time."

"There's something wrong with you if you don't like Christmas. And bring Rocko. We love him."

Meredith may be right. There might be something wrong with me. But it's not that I don't like Christmas, it's just that I would rather be on my own while the rest of the world goes crazy; eats too much; gets gifts they don't want; watches sappy stupid movies. And don't get me started on Christmas songs. I can't stand Michael Bublé and Mariah Carey and all the rest of those Christmas classics on high rotation in every store in every mall. The whole tinsel-covered commercial con makes me want to run and hide.

"If I wasn't stuck up at the mansion." I point in the general direction. "I'd be far far away, somewhere where Christmas doesn't even exist."

"Scrooge."

"Yes. That's exactly what I mean."

"Grump."

"And again. Is the next one going to be Grinch?"

"Yes. How did you guess?" Meredith hugs me. "The invitation is there if you want it. Anytime. We love you. Now get lost, soldier."

"Bah. Humbug. And it's ex-soldier, again."

"I know. I just like needling you."

Meredith is my kid sister, but she has always seemed older and wiser than me. I trust her more than anyone else in the world. And I don't like to disappoint, but Christmas is not my friend. The whole holly-jolly shebang makes me nauseous. And anxious.

Every year it's like watching a parade from the sidelines. I don't get how people are so invested in something so commercial and trite. I'm planning to have a nice time with Rocko without sleigh bells or snow.

I climb back into the Chevy and drum the steering wheel. Focus on the positive. Key in the ignition. Get my head down and get the mansion ready for a quick sale. Turn the key, start up the engine, and back out of the driveway. Sell the mansion and I'm free.

On the way out of town, I remember to pick up a few things from the supermarket. Dog food mostly. But it's a good idea to go shopping when I happen to be in town. Living at the mansion means it's inconvenient to run out of anything when it's a thirty-minute drive to the nearest store.

At the supermarket, I sit for a minute in the busy parking lot, mentally preparing myself, as if I'm on a military exercise. Then, like a bullet from a gun, I'm in through the sliding doors, blotting out the inane jolly songs that assault me at full volume. I ignore the oversized grinning Santas and twinkly-colored festive lights. Every product seems to have holly or mistletoe pictured, or an elf or reindeer. I charge up and down each aisle, avoiding collisions with families and their shopping carts, gathering what I need at breakneck speed to get to the row of checkouts as fast as possible. I assess which line to join and stand patiently, inching forward, until it's my turn.

The checkout operator is wearing a Santa hat and Christmas tree earrings and has a snowman painted on her cheek. She twinkles at me as she scans my items.

"Do you have plans for the holidays?" she asks with a friendly smile.

"No. Not really." I'm in no mood to chat.

"Do you have a Jolly Holly Holiday Christmas discount card, sir?"

"No. I don't."

"Well, would you like one? It'll give you ten percent off your purchases from now until the end of January. All you do is fill out the form with your details and..."

"No. No, thank you," I say abruptly cutting her off.

The checkout operator purses her lips, takes my bank card, and swipes it through the machine.

"Well. Did you hear? There's a storm coming. The weather channel has issued a warning. Severe is what's expected. Looks like we're in for a white Christmas." She beams. "Now that's something to be cheerful about, isn't it?"

She hands my card back to me with a receipt and bats her eyelashes.

"Thanks." I am trying to be cheerful, but I know that I'm gritting my teeth with the effort.

"Merry Christmas, sir. I hope to see you again soon."

I grab my bags and get out of there as quickly as I can. Once safely back in my truck, I take a deep breath and hope that I haven't forgotten anything.

The last place I want to be is a busy supermarket at Christmastime. The flashing lights remind me of emergency strobes and the tinny electronic sounds are too much like sirens. But I relax knowing that I have enough supplies for a few days if a storm does blow through. And, thankfully, I don't need to endure another shopping trip until the silly season is well and truly over. Who knows how long the storm will last? But then I'll be snowed in and have a valid excuse for not showing up for Christmas at Meredith's.

With these happy thoughts in my head, I drive back up the hill to the mansion, noticing how heavy the sky is and how it is getting darker by the minute. Definitely looks like a storm's coming. I turn onto Belleview Road. It's quiet. There's no other traffic which is not unusual. Even when the traffic on the main highway is at a standstill, there's no real advantage to driving this way.

As I approach the mansion's driveway, I see the fairy in the ladybug still sitting where I left her. I slow down, pull over, stop, and get out.

"Hey. I'm surprised that you're still here." I zip up my jacket. The temperature has plummeted.

"Yeah. Me too." The fairy winds down her window. "I shouldn't have to wait too much longer. I hope." She holds up a hand with her fingers crossed, smiles, and shivers slightly.

"Well, okay." Then, without thinking, I follow up with, "Why not wait at my place? It's just around this corner, up that driveway." I point up the hill. "You could call the roadside guys and tell them to meet you there."

"Oh, that's kind of you. But I think I'll stay put. I have everything I need here. It's fine. I'm not going to be here long."

"Well, if you're sure."

"Yes. I'm sure. But thanks, again."

"Look. If you change your mind, I'm right around the corner in the big house, The Mansion Hotel. Take my number. I'll come and get you."

"I appreciate your offer, but I'm fine. Really."

"Okay, then. Take care."

The fairy winds up her window to end the conversation. I look up and down the empty road, then back away to my truck. She is a grown adult person who can make her own decisions. But I can't help but be protective. It's in my nature. I will stop by in a couple of hours to make sure she is still okay or gone.

Chapter 4

Charlie

I watch Mr Gorgeous Single Dad drive away and I can't quite believe I turned down his offer. I thump the steering wheel and slap my own stupid face. Why didn't I just go with him? It would have been so easy to say, "Yes, please. I would love to wait at your place for the breakdown service, and not all alone at the stupid side of the road." But I am too proud to admit that I need help. And to put myself in another more awkward situation where I am close to a man who is absolutely gorgeous and absolutely out of bounds.

I'd rather stay in my stupid broken chilly car than get in his late-model Chevy with functioning heating and go back to his happy home and meet his equally gorgeous wife and perfect family in their big old fancy house in a manicured park up their private driveway. No thank you.

"I'm fine. Really," I say bravely knowing that the breakdown guys are delayed because of an accident on the main highway. They called to tell me.

The hot guy gets into his truck and, thankfully, drives away before I cave in and change my mind.

Oh, man. I peer out of the windshield at the ominous heavy grey sky. It's going to be dark soon. However, the day has never properly woken up, like a lazy person who stays in their pajamas from breakfast until bedtime.

And I am seriously running out of patience. I've been waiting for hours for Roadside Recovery and I'm still here. I feel like a prize chump.

Lou calls back. She says that she'll come get me, but I tell her no; that someone will be with me soon; that according to Roadside Recovery and Insurance, I am a priority customer.

"I'll be fine," I say looking out of the window at the scudding clouds overhead. "I'm watching the birds, and you'll never guess what..." I was going to mention the hot dad from Isabel's party but think better of it because she would want to know every last detail about him and that would surely use up what's left of my battery. "... I've just seen a fox!"

"Yay! Wildlife."

"Yes." I sigh. "I am making the best of the situation. Finding the positive. Smiling in the face of defeat. The world is still a beautiful place, my friend."

"You got this, Charlie."

"Yes, I have, Lou. Look, I'll see you soon. Muah!" And with that, I hang up the call.

I'm bright and breezy when I say goodbye, cutting the call short because my phone battery dropped below ten percent. As I hang up, I think, if I'm so prioritized with Roadside Recovery, then how come I am still here at the side of the road? But talking with my friend has elevated my flagging spirits and shone a spotlight on a situation that really isn't that bad. I take a moment to breathe and focus on what I'm learning from this experience.

I am a firm believer of *Fake it til you make it* philosophy and the physiological fact that you can change your mood and frame of mind by smiling: pretending that you're happy until you actually are. It's simple but it works.

I'm grinning like a Cheshire cat as a soft misty rain begins to fog up Bertie's windows. Thinking happy thoughts, I hear the soft misty rain increase in intensity and gently drum on the roof.

My phone rings. I pick up instantly.

"Mr Charlie Lennox?"

"It's Miss, actually."

"Hi. Miss. This is Roadside Recovery. I'm sorry to have to inform you that we can't get a recovery vehicle out to you tonight due to road closure in the area. All our recovery vehicles are deployed at this present time. We're doing our utmost in these circumstances…"

"What? Can't get to me tonight? That is unacceptable. What the…"

"Sorry ma'am. I know this is inconvenient. The best we can do is tomorrow morning."

"No. No. No, no, no. I'm in the middle of nowhere."

"Is there someone you can call?"

"Yes." I close my eyes. "Yes, thank you… I'll do that."

"Please stay on the line and rate our customer service. Your feedback is imp…"

My phone dies before the end of the sentence.

The drumming rain gets heavier and louder. I'll wait until it stops. Then I'll… What? My options have dwindled to one.

I pack as much as I can into my bag and locate my umbrella, which thankfully, is where I thought it might be, stashed under the seat. The rain has not eased up but is getting heavier and turning to sleet, which attacks me on an aggressive diagonal when the car door is whipped open by a sharp gust of wind, as I clamber out. I fumble with the umbrella, which doesn't want to cooperate, and I pull my faux fur jacket tight around me wishing it was a more practical piece of wet weather gear. My sparkly ballet pumps leak instantly and bone-aching cold sets in.

I lock up the broken car and stomp off up the road to find the turning to the hot guy's house. Determined not to let things get me down, I put on my happy face and look on the bright side, as I slosh through freezing puddles. At least, when I get to the hotel, I can charge up my phone and call Lou to come and get me. This really is my only option now.

By the time I arrive at the wrought-iron gate, my dress is soaked through, and my faux fur jacket is acting like a sponge. I wrestle with my umbrella which has blown inside out a couple of times in the ever-increasing biting wind. I can't feel my feet anymore.

The double gate is chained together, which isn't very welcoming for guests arriving at the hotel. I search the ivy-covered walls on either side for a button to press, but there isn't one. I grab the gate with both hands and shake it vigorously. I call out, but my voice is whisked away by the wind and drowned by rain. The roof of a small house or a shed is behind a dense bush close by. I call out again, louder this time, and a massive dog comes hurtling around the corner and jumps up at the gate in front of me growling and barking fiercely. I'm so shocked I scream and drop my umbrella which instantly blows away.

"Rocko. Down boy," a man says as my phone drops out of my pocket and splashes into a puddle when I bend down and scrabble around trying to retrieve the inside-out umbrella. "Don't be scared. He's a big softy. Aren't you, boy."

I drag my hair off my face and blink the rain out of my eyes to see Mr Gorgeous Dad lifting the weighty chain and pulling it through to open one of the gates.

"Come on in," he shouts through the deluge.

Rocko stands to attention to let me pass. The hot guy closes the gate behind us and repositions the chain but doesn't lock it. I follow him around a corner to a teeny tiny house that wouldn't look out of place in a Disney movie about princesses and evil stepmothers. Mr Gorgeous Dad takes off his raincoat under the porch and gives it a shake. Then ushers me in, shuts the door behind me, and hangs his coat on a peg in the hall. Inside is warm, dry, and relatively quiet after being out in the rain which still insistently hits the roof and windows.

"Hey, thanks so much. The recovery guys can't come for me until tomorrow," I say with teeth chattering. "Can you believe it? I'm not going to be awarding many stars on their customer service feedback form, that's for sure."

"Is this what you have for your emergency kit? A fake fur and an umbrella?"

"Excuse me?"

"Well, if you're driving any distance, it's a good idea to be prepared for all kinds of emergency."

"Thanks. Well, I did have roadside emergency cover, but that has clearly let me down." I follow the hot guy into a tiny living room which is warm and cozy, so I forgive him for lecturing me. "So, if I can please charge up my phone I'll call my friend, and she can come and get me. She's only an hour away. Maybe a bit more, but…"

"Sure." The hot guy takes my phone and wipes it on his sleeve. "But it looks a bit wet. You might need to dry it out before plugging it into the mains."

I feel myself physically sag as he says this. My energy saps away by the second.

"You're right." I take the phone back and wipe it on my sodden jacket. It's a futile act. The phone gets wetter.

"I'm Jason by the way," says the hot guy holding out a hand for me to shake. "I'll get you a towel. You should get out of those wet things. Hyperthermia is real and dangerous in these circumstances."

"Oh yes. Right," I say taking off my jacket which drips on the floor. Jason disappears through a door on the other side of the room by the fireplace.

Rocko is curled up on a wingback chair. He's off-duty and snoozing. I take in the furnishings of the tiny space which doesn't look as if it has been decorated for a hundred years. The wood stove is set beneath a carved wooden surround. Everything in the room is old. I feel like I'm in a museum or a living exhibit which gives a visitor an authentic taste of yesteryear. Jason comes back holding out a towel for me.

I take it gratefully and rub the towel over my head and dry my face, but suddenly I remember my fairy make-up of mostly pink glitter, which transfers to the snowy-white towel.

"Sorry."

"Don't worry about it." Jason rolls his eyes then says, "I'm going to get you a hot drink. Sweet coffee."

"No sugar thanks." I wrap the towel around my shivering shoulders.

"Not sugar. Honey. It'll give you an energy burst without spiking your insulin." He begins to walk to the other door in the room but stops mid-stride. "I'll wring this out over the kitchen sink," he says taking my soggy faux fur with a derisive smirk. "I can't imagine a more impractical jacket in this weather."

As Jason turns to leave, I forgive yet another lecture and I listen as he fills the kettle.

"Well, Jason. I didn't think I was going to be hiking in a snowstorm when I left my house this morning," I shout after him.

"You need a decent jacket. Waterproof. Padded. Something you can sleep out in, if necessary," Jason says as he comes back into the lounge, shaking my substandard fake fur and arranging it on the arm of Rocko's chair beside the fire.

"Thanks," I say looking around, trying to formulate a plan. I'm still chilled but warming up a little.

"Alright. Here's what I think we should do," says Jason with a serious expression, combing his fingers through his dark wavy hair - an action so captivating, it takes my mind off my horrendous predicament. "First, we should see if we can get your car started. I have jumper cables, so that might be all that's needed. But before we go out there again, you need to put on some dry clothes."

"Oh, I'm fine," I say, my voice juddering with shivers. "And I don't have anything dry."

"I do. What I suggest is you take a hot shower to warm up. I'll sort out something for you to wear. Then, by that time, your phone should be dry enough to plug in and it'll be charging while we're getting your car sorted out. How does that sound?"

"Are you Jason Bates? Is this the Bates Hotel? I've seen Psycho and I know what happens to the lady in the shower."

Chapter 5

Jason

Charlie perches on my couch and looks around the room, taking in the wallpaper, pictures, and framed photos. Her eyes come to rest on Rocko who is snoring peacefully on the chair in front of the wood stove. I get the feeling she is weighing up my suggestion of a shower and change of clothes.

"If this was a horror movie, something dreadful is going to happen next," she says followed by a nervous laugh.

"Are you kidding?"

"Jason. I'm going to ask you straight out. Are you an ax murderer?"

"Mmmm. I see your point. What if I tell you that nothing bad is going to happen? I'm just trying to help." Charlie shivers. She sips the hot coffee but doesn't move at all. Her eyes dart to the door. She's thinking about an exit plan, I'll bet. "If it'll make you feel better, I'll call my sister, Meredith, and she'll tell you I'm a good guy, okay?"

Charlie nods, pulls the towel tighter around her shoulders, and sips more coffee. I dial Meredith's number. The phone rings a couple of times before she picks up.

"Hey, Meredith. I have a guest here who needs you to give me a character reference. Alright?"

"Hey, Jase. What's going on?"

"Meredith. Please tell Charlie, here, that I'm a good guy."

"Charlie? Boy or girl?"

I breathe deeply and feel a little bashful. "Girl." I sit down next to Charlie.

"Ah, Jason. It's so great that you're dating."

"No Meredith. Not dating. I just rescued Charlie at the side of the road. She thinks I'm an ax murderer."

"Okay. Put her on." I hand my phone to Charlie. Her pink sparkly dress drips on the carpet.

"Alright, Charlie?" Meredith's voice is clear. Charlie says hello. Then my helpful sister says, "Run and keep running." Charlie's eyes ping wide open in shock. She jumps up, spilling her coffee. "Only kidding. Jason's my big brother. Ask me anything you'd like to know."

"Ha! Meredith." Charlie laughs, putting the mug on the floor and brushing the spilled coffee from her skirt. "You almost had me. Thanks for the scare."

"Sorry. Just my sense of humor. But really, Jason is a bit rough around the edges and he may come across as a total grump but he's the sweetest, nicest..." I take back my phone before Meredith gets too carried away.

"Thanks, Meredith. I think I've got it from here." I hang up the call.

Rocko lifts his head and blinks at me. The wind is picking up. Leafless branches thrash around outside the window. My dog grumbles, yawns, and goes back to sleep.

Charlie picks up the coffee mug and holds it with both hands. She's still shivering but I can tell that she has relaxed a little.

"Maybe you need to call someone? You can use my phone while yours is out of action."

"That would be..." I hand Charlie my phone. She smiles. "My roommates will be worrying now. Thank you," she says. Then she looks at the ceiling and laughs. "I don't know Lou's number. I only ever call on speed dial." She thinks for a minute. "No. Wait. It's on the website. Could you help me?"

"Sure." I take back my phone.

"My friend's number is on the Sparkle Entertainers website." I type the name into the search engine and Sparkle Entertainers is at the top of the results page.

"Is this it?"

"Yup. Okay." Charlie sits close beside me as I scroll down to the end of the colorful homepage showing an array of photos: jugglers, clowns, stilt-walkers, wizards, and fairies.

"Ah, is that you?" I say pointing at a pretty pink fairy with beautiful wings and a wand, blowing enormous bubbles.

"Yes." Charlie beams at me. "That was at Coachella a couple of years ago. So much fun, I can't begin to tell you."

"Coachella?"

"The festival? Not as big as Burning Man, or Bonnaroo, but it's right up there for me. And that year, we had the best time. I forget who was headlining but when the vibe is buzzing and everyone is on the same wave, it doesn't matter, does it?"

"I guess not."

"What's your favorite festie, then? No. Let me guess. South By Southwest? Something more C and W?"

"C and W?"

"Country and western. Stagecoach, say? Or maybe you're into jazz in which case New Orleans would be your bag."

"My bag?"

"Yes. What you're into."

"What I'm into."

"Yes. Gosh Jason. Coachella is hands down the best way to spend three days."

"I'm sorry. You've lost me."

"Don't tell me you've never heard about the best festival in the entire world? Where have you been?"

"Peacekeeping for the United Nations."

"Oh. Right. In that case, you're forgiven. But you should go one year. It's... Well, just go."

"Alright. Maybe I will." There's a moment before I say, "So, here's the number. I'll dial it for you if you want."

"Yes please."

"It's ringing." As Charlie takes my phone, I notice how her eyes are sparkling behind the smeared mascara and smudged eyeliner. She really is very pretty.

"Thanks," she says smiling warmly which causes my pulse to race. I swallow hard.

"I'll be in the kitchen." I walk away to get a grip on myself and to give her some privacy. Lou could be her boyfriend for all I know. They might be serious. She could be engaged to Lou. I don't even know why that matters. It doesn't. I hear snippets of her conversation in the kitchen. She says things like 'don't worry' and 'I'm fine' and 'I'll tell you all about it when I see you'. Are these the sorts of things you say to your fiancé?

I realize that I'm eavesdropping, so I wash some dishes and tidy things on shelves, and think about what to cook. Something hot. A soup maybe.

Charlie ends the call and smiles at me from the doorway.

"Lou's going to come and get me, no worries. Calvin's coming too. They'll be a couple of hours which is alright, isn't it?"

"Sure. That's fine with me." I open the fridge. "I'm going to cook some food," I say over my shoulder. "You're welcome to share. Is there anything you don't eat?"

"Thanks for asking. I'm actually starving, but I'm vegetarian. Is that a problem?"

"Not at all. I'm not, but I can make a meat-free noodle soup. Something like that? Would that be okay?" I close the fridge door and lean on the kitchen counter, aware of the feeling of contentment in cooking for Charlie, and the idea that we have a couple of hours together.

"Perfect. Thanks." Charlie stands framed by the doorway. Her make up is smudged, her damp hair chaotic. Pink glitter sparkles. She's pretty as a picture. I realize that I'm staring and lower my gaze.

"I'll show you where the bathroom is," I say remembering that Charlie must be dying for a shower. I lead her from the kitchen through the living room to the bathroom. "Help yourself to whatever's there. Shampoo, um. Anything, you know." I turn the handle and push open the door for her.

"Oh, goodness. Look at me!" Charlie sees her reflection in the mirror above the hand basin. "What an absolute mess." Her hands smooth down her bedraggled hair.

"You're alright." I laugh. "Anyway. Take your time. I'll sort out some dry clothes and leave them outside the door for you." I turn to leave but Charlie stops me.

"Jason." She lifts her chin to regain some dignity, then says, "Thank you for rescuing me and for not being a psycho ax murderer. That would have been the icing of disaster on the cake of catastrophe today."

"You're welcome."

"I'm still going to lock the door."

"You can't. There's no lock."

"Alright then. See you in a minute."

Charlie closes the bathroom door, and I go to my bedroom. I open the closet to find some warm clothes for my fairy guest. I surprise myself by considering what she might like: plaid or plain? Grey or blue? T-shirt or shirt? I hold a shirt in each hand but then I decide on a selection and allow Charlie to choose. Everything will be oversized on her, but my track pants have a drawstring at the waist, and she can roll them up at the ankles. I find a pair of thick hiking socks, but I don't have any shoes that are going to fit. Never mind. We'll figure something out.

I hear the shower running and Charlie singing as I leave the pile of clothes outside the bathroom door. In the living room, her ridiculous fake fur jacket still drips on the rug. I take it to the kitchen and wring it out again, more thoroughly this time, before giving it a shake and arranging it to dry on a coat hanger.

Pink glitter seems to be everywhere. It's on the carpet. It's on the couch and the chairs. It's even on Rocko. And it's on me. It's a biohazard, an environmental debacle. I decide to vacuum when Charlie moves on to fairyland or wherever she's going.

In the kitchen, I take some vegetables from the fridge and find a packet of noodles. I could make a stir-fry or a mee goreng. Something hot and nourishing. Maybe a curry laksa. I have most of the ingredients.

I hear the bathroom door open and Charlie yelling out a 'thank you' before she shuts the door again.

I chop the vegetables into small pieces and heat up some oil in a wok. It's simple food. There's not much to it. Malaysian tasty soup is quick and delicious. I hope Charlie likes it. If she doesn't, I have some eggs. I could make scrambled eggs. Maybe poached.

Rocko waddles into the kitchen and snuffles around just to make sure I haven't dropped any tasty morsels. He slurps a messy drink from his water bowl and ambles back to the warmth of the living room.

"Hey." Charlie stands in the doorway wearing my clothes. She's small and swamped beneath layers of T-shirt, shirt, and a woolen sweater. "I feel so much better. Thanks for the clothes. Gosh. And thanks for not bursting in with that big knife and slicing me to pieces."

"No problem. Should I do it now?" I say holding up the kitchen knife.

"Ha. You're funny."

"But blood is so hard to clean up. Maybe I'll just poison you with my Malaysian curry laksa."

"Smells delicious. I'll risk being poisoned."

"Are you sure you wouldn't prefer eggs lightly scrambled on sourdough?"

"No, really. Curry laksa is perfect."

"I guessed that you're a vege," I say stirring the chopped carrot, broccoli, onions, and cabbage in the oil. They sizzle and spit. "Before you told me."

"Oh, really? Am I that obvious and easy to read?"

"Yup. Let me see now. Fairy. Drives a VW Beetle painted to look like a ladybug. I'd say chances are high that she's a vegetarian with hippy tendencies."

"Yes. You're right. One hundred percent." Charlie comes closer and watches as I stir the can of coconut milk through the vegetables in the wok. "What can I do?"

"You can get some bowls out from the shelf there and spoons are in that drawer." I point with my elbow. "You look almost human without your pink glittery makeup."

"Ah, yes. I forget that I'm wearing it sometimes." Charlie puts the bowls and two spoons on the bench top. "Just us for food, then? Or is your daughter joining?"

"My daughter?"

"The little girl in the truck with you when you stopped the first time?"

"Ha! No. I mean. Maddie. She's my niece. She's Meredith's daughter. I was on uncle duty this morning."

"Okay. That clears up that question… I thought you… Never mind."

"Curry's almost ready." I use a ladle to scoop out a portion into one of the bowls then I hand it to Charlie.

"We can eat in the living room. It's the warmest place. Go make yourself comfortable."

I spoon out a bowlful for me and follow Charlie into the cozy lounge. She sits cross-legged on the couch next to Rocko and I sit on the chair opposite. The fire crackles and my inherited property headache floats away. For a while, I forget about my financial burden. A fairy is in my house, and she is lovely.

Chapter 6

Charlie

Jason's curry laksa noodle soup is piping hot and delicious. The heat of the soup and the chili heat warm me to my toes so much so, I pause eating to take off Jason's homespun sweater. I sit cross-legged on the couch. Jason sits in the chair opposite. We're quiet while we eat. Although I am aware of the noise I'm making as I slurp my noodles and of appearing less than cultured in the company of my fine-looking host. Sleet hits the window and the wind howls down the chimney.

"When we're done," Jason says. "We'll go and take a look at your car."

"Great."

"I have another rain jacket, so you don't get soaked again. And you can try my hiking boots. They're going to be way too big, but they'll keep your feet warm and dry out there."

"Thanks." My nose is running with the heat of the spicy soup, so I get some tissue from the bathroom. In the steamed-up mirror, I see how my cheeks are rosy like a painted doll's. I mop up a dribble of laksa from my chin and congratulate myself on being the messiest eater in the world.

"You okay in there?"

"Yeah. I always seem to wear my food," I shout through the door. "It's the reason I'm still single," I say to my reflection before returning to the living room.

Jason has collected the bowls and taken them to the kitchen.

"All set?" he says holding out a raincoat for me.

"Sure."

Rocko jumps down from the chair and wags his tail.

"You stay here, boy." Jason smooshes Rocko's face between his hands then strokes the animal's enormous head.

"I have some tools in the truck. But I won't know what to do until I look under the hood."

"Are you a mechanic?"

"Engineer. It's about the same thing. I usually work on really big engines. That's about the only difference."

Outside, Jason pulls his hood over his head against the horizontal sleet and dashes to the gate to open it up. I climb into the cab of the Chevy and Jason joins me soon after. In the short time of being outside our raincoats are slick with water.

"I hope Bertie hasn't blown away in the storm."

"Bertie?"

"My car. His name is Bertie the Beetle."

"Of course it is." Jason laughs then starts the Chevy and reverses out of the gate.

It only takes a few minutes to drive down the narrow lane that seemed to go on forever when I was walking up it earlier. Bertie is, thankfully, still there waiting, forlorn and broken, at the side of the road.

"Okay. You pop the hood, and I'll have a look," Jason says reaching for a toolbox behind the driver's seat.

I don't want to get out of the warm dry cab, but Jason is already at the front of Bertie waiting for me to unlock the door and pop the hood. I take a deep breath then make a dash for my car, get the key in the lock, and open the door. I throw myself onto the driver's seat.

Inside Bertie smells of musty damp mixed with strawberry hair product. Every surface is sprinkled with pink glitter. I pull the rain jacket hood over my head and join Jason at the engine. He looks serious and wipes his oily hands on a rag.

"We'll try the jumper cables," Jason shouts above the din of the lashing rain. "But I'm sorry to say that it's maybe something more than a dead battery."

I stand to one side as Jason attaches the red and black cables to the battery points in Bertie's engine, then he opens the hood of the Chevy and clips them on in there too. His progress is hampered by sideways rain that blows in bucketloads. I think I'll need another hot shower and a change of clothes after this episode, and I've only been standing out here for a few minutes. Jason jumps into the driver's seat and starts up the Chevy. He pumps the accelerator which makes the engine roar.

"Hey, Charlie. You're getting soaked again. Hop in, out of the rain."

Jason's sensible suggestion clicks me out of my mental fog, and I scurry round to the passenger door of the Chevy, open it, and hop inside.

"This storm is getting worse," says Jason as he turns on the radio which is playing the Christmas classic, 'All I Want For Christmas Is You'. "We should get a weather update soon."

"I love this one!" I can't help singing along and dancing in my seat. I expect Jason to join in with the chorus, but he just stares at me.

"Come on, Jason. Sing it with feeling, 'All I want for Christmas is you!'" I belt out the lyrics at the top of my lungs as if I am possessed by the spirit of Mariah Carey. Jason blinks and sighs patiently. I feel self-conscious and stop singing. "Alright. Well, maybe not this particular Christmas song but the next one? We'll see, huh?"

The next song is Boney M, 'Mary's Boychild'.

"Ah, no. This one's not one of my favorites." Jason fixes me with an accusatory stare as if I am the ax murderer. I shrug and stare back. "What?"

"Here we are, at the side of the road, in a storm, and you're singing along to Christmas songs?"

"Yeah. Tis the season to be jolly, falalalalah-lala-la-lah. Where's your Christmas spirit?" Jason blows out another long sigh. "Alright. What's your favorite song, then?"

"I don't have a favorite. They're all garbage." He shakes his head. "I don't really like Christmas. At all."

I gasp. "Don't like Christmas?" And I'm about to follow up with, "What is wrong with you?" but I remember my manners, and that Jason is rescuing me, so I smile and say, "Did you have a bad Christmas experience growing up?"

"No. Why do you say that?"

"No reason." I stare straight ahead. "Just a vibe I'm getting."

"A vibe."

"Yes. It's... I'm sensitive to a person's energy. You know, their aura."

Jason starts laughing. "You are one out of box, alright, fairy. Unique. There's only one of you, right? At least I hope that's the case."

"Oh. Okay. I get it. I appreciate you helping me. And I'll remember to keep my opinions to myself."

The song finishes and the announcer comes on.

"Looks like we're all set for a white Christmas, folks."

I squeal with excitement and clap my hands. "Yay!" Jason rolls his eyes at me.

The radio guy continues. "The latest from the weather office is this. A blizzard is due to strike in the next few hours, so here's what the emergency services advise. Number one: stay home. Do not travel. Number two: make sure you have candles and flashlights ready and waiting in preparation for a power outage. Number three: look after each other. Hunker down. This is going to be a big one."

"Oooh. That's not good." I bite my lip. My earlier enthusiasm is squashed like a bug.

The radio announcer continues, "In case you just joined us, the latest weather report is rated as code red. That's code R.E.D., everyone. Stay home. Stay safe. We'll be here to keep you updated. Now, another Christmas classic from The Ronettes, 'Frosty the Snowman'." As the intro of Phil Spector's unmistakable tune begins to play, the announcer says with zeal, "Ha! There's going to be a whole heap of snow soon, so stand by, Frosty. You're sure to get a whole lot of snow buddies. Ho, ho, ho! Merry Christmas, everybody."

"Oh, boy." Jason clenches his jaw. The Chevy engine is still running but the charge of energy has disappeared from the inside of the cab. "Do you want to try and get Bertie going? I mean, if he's up to it, you could still get to the city before the storm hits."

"It's worth a go," I say with my perkiest, brightest smile as I open the door and prepare to dart out to my car, although the oversized hiking boots threaten to trip me up.

I take a deep breath then scamper, as if moving fast is going to make a difference to how wet I get. I open Bertie's driver's door and climb in. Jason watches through the windshield of the Chevy in front. I can just about see him behind the open hood of my ancient Beetle. I hear the Chevy's engine rev, and I send up a prayer to the gods of car mechanics as turn the key in Bertie's ignition.

Click.

Nothing. I try it again, foolishly expecting a different outcome.

Click.

Jason shuts off the Chevy and mimes a throat slice, the international signal for 'Stop what you are doing. It's useless. Everything is useless.' He jumps out of the cab and splashes over to remove the jumper cables from Bertie, and then unclips them from the battery in the Chevy. I get out and join him in the sideways rain.

"It didn't work."

"No."

"What now?" I shout over the increasing noise of wind and rain. Jason waves me in the direction of the Chevy. He coils the jumper cables and jumps into the driver's seat. I clamber in the passenger side and take off my hood.

"Here's my suggestion," says Jason turning toward me. Rain drips from his beard. He wipes it away with the back of his hand.

"Okay. Go ahead. I'm all ears," I say, although I'm thinking about Jason's beard and how nice it would be to run my fingers through.

"I'll tow you back to the hotel. I'm guessing the roadside recovery guys won't be out tomorrow because of the code-red weather warning. You can call them to update your location and status. That way you will be removed from the search and rescue critical list, otherwise emergency crews will be out looking for you, okay?"

"Sure. If that's alright. Then, let's do it."

Jason nods. "Right. Here's what we're going to do next. Your car…"

"Bertie."

"Yes, Bertie, needs to be facing the other way." Jason points up the hill toward the hotel. "So, you're going to steer. And I'll push. Got it?"

"Yep."

"Okay. So, the road isn't wide enough to push it round in one go. We need to make a three-point turn. Forward, back, then forward again."

"I know what a three-point turn is." I get the feeling that Jason thinks I'm an imbecile.

"I just need to be clear because we're doing this together. We're a team, Charlie."

"Alright," I say opening the door. "Let's do this."

I run to Bertie's driver's door and throw myself in. Jason runs to the back and taps on the roof to let me know that he's ready. I release the handbrake and slowly I feel my little car crawl forward. I pull the steering wheel over as far as I can. Before I hit the bank on the other side of the road, Jason taps the roof again. Then he sprints round to the front and heaves Bertie backwards with me steering the opposite way this time. Another tap on the roof and Jason is at the back again pushing Bertie with all his might but we hardly make any headway because of the upwards incline. Jason taps the roof then appears at my window. I wind it down to hear what he has to say.

"I'm going to push you back down the hill, so steer over behind the Chevy. Careful to cover your brake, in case you pick up too much speed. You don't want to end up in the ditch."

I nod and wind the window up as Jason gets in front and leans onto the hood. The slight gradient works in our favor this time and I easily coast backward to smoothly rest behind Jason's truck.

I look for Jason, to see if I get the thumbs up for a job well done, but he has disappeared. In a moment he returns from the Chevy's cab with a coil of rope. Without hesitation, he drops to the ground and secures the rope hook somewhere on Bertie's underside. It makes a scraping noise and a vibration beneath my feet. He then jumps up and masterfully takes the other end and hooks it to the rear end of the Chevy. In a moment he's back at my window.

"Alright, Charlie. Have you been towed before? I'm guessing yes."

"Why yes?" I'm indignant at the assumption.

"Because of the car you drive. It's old. Anyway..."

"Yes. Yes, I've been towed before, so... Shall we?"

"Just hold your foot over the brake," Jason shouts with authority. "I know we're mostly going uphill, but I don't want you to rear-end my truck, okay? Although, I think Bertie would come off much worse than the big old Chevy."

"Sure. Got it. It's not that far. What could possibly go wrong?"

"Charlie, that is not a question you should be asking." Jason straightens up and taps Bertie's roof. "Ready?"

"Ready."

I wind up the window and prepare to steer, still feeling prickly about Jason's bossiness. But I let it go because he's helping me out. Big time. And also, I'm a bit overwhelmed with his handsome heroics. No one has ever thrown themselves on the wet cold ground at my feet before. I get the sense that he is quite the capable man and, if I was attracted to him before this moment, I am actually falling in love now. But he does have an attitude and also, he's more than a little negative, especially around Christmas and fairies. But we can work on that when we…

"Okay, Charlie?" Jason shouts before he gets into the Chevy.

I toot Bertie's horn a couple of times and wave although I'm pretty sure Jason isn't looking.

The Chevy's taillights blaze in the gloom, as Jason slowly pulls away. The tow rope extends out straight then I feel the tug as it pulls on my car. Then I remember to release the handbrake, and I jolt forward as if I've been kicked from behind.

"Oops."

The rope slackens off as Jason makes the turn, his hazard lights blink an orange warning which is amplified through the rain-splattered window, although no one is on the road to see them, or likely to be.

Chapter 7

Jason

My plan to release the fairy back into the wild fell flat at the radio announcement of the incoming blizzard. The DJ was fizzy with delight as he said the words 'code red' as if he was announcing a prize giveaway. Anyway. It's fine. What are my choices? The window of opportunity to, Option A, get the ancient VW started so Charlie could drive away to where she came from; or, Option B, to drive her to wherever she wanted to go - has slammed shut with a resounding bang.

I was fully prepared to take her to her boyfriend's place. Family. Her downtown apartment. I don't know. Somewhere away from here. Now, it seems, we are stuck here to wait out the storm together. It's a good thing I stopped by the supermarket on the way back from Meredith's. I'm pretty sure we have enough supplies for two or three days, if it comes to that.

As I slowly drive through the gate, the sleet has turned to snow. My windshield wipers slosh from side to side at double speed but fail to clear the snow build-up fast enough. I park close to the gatehouse, cut the engine, and jump out. I wave at Charlie, although her windshield and windows are almost completely covered in snow. I'm not sure how much she can see so I tap the VW roof as I stride to the gate, push it shut, and secure the chain which is icy to touch. The wind gusts and throws the snow around. It stings my face, and my fingers are numb with cold. Charlie is at the front door waiting for me, hopping from one foot to the other.

"It's not locked. Go on in," I tell her, surprised that she's still outside in the freezing porch.

"After you," she yells above the din of the storm. "Rocko might eat me."

Rocko is in the hall to greet us. He pushes his head into my hand and leans against my legs. Charlie takes off the rain jacket.

"He's not going to eat you. He might lick you to death." I take the rain jacket from her and shake it outside before hanging it up. "It might be different if you were trying to break in. Uninvited. But he knows you're my guest, so you're safe."

Charlie unties the oversized hiking boots and kicks them off. I peel out of my rain jacket, shake it, then hang it on the coat rack too. I take off my boots. The storm rages outside furiously rattling the doors and windows.

"I had no idea the storm would come in so fast and fierce," says Charlie heading for the wood stove to warm her hands.

"It's frightening, alright. But we're safe now." I bend down to open the stove door and place a large log inside.

"Yeah, we're safe until the roof blows off," Charlie says rubbing her hands together and stamping her feet.

"You're right but this little house is solid, and we're sheltered behind the wall. So, unless a tree falls on us, we'll be okay."

"Ha! You're so casual about it."

"I don't think it's something to worry about. Think about it. How many storms have blown through here since this place was built around one hundred and fifty years ago? It's still standing. We'll be okay." It's important to keep calm. I hope I have reassured my guest of our safety as I close the door and straighten up. "We have enough dry wood, I think, and electric heaters." I stand beside Charlie and warm my hands too. "I'm pretty sure I bought candles and new batteries for the flashlights. I'll go check."

I leave Charlie at the fireside and find batteries, three flashlights, and box of candles, a lighter, and a box of matches in one of the kitchen cupboards. I leave them on the kitchen countertop, then I come back to the living room.

"How are you? Not too wet?" I ask Charlie whose cheeks are glowing pink. "Are you cold?"

"No. I'm okay although I could change the track pants, if you have another pair?" she says holding the wet fabric out from her legs on either side. They look like elephant ears. "The rest of me is dry as a bone. That's a good rain jacket you have there."

"Thanks, I know."

"Better than fake fur any day." Charlie laughs as I walk past her to my room to find another pair of track pants. When I come back, she takes the folded dry pants from me as if they are sacred and says, "Thanks for lending me the clothes. I'll return them when I check in to one of the rooms. I guess there will be a robe for me or something warm I can put on."

"Sorry. What?"

"The hotel." Charlie looks at me, puzzled. "That is what the sign says." She points out of the window toward the big old house. "I'll stay at the hotel tonight. One of the rooms? I hope they have a vacancy for me. I didn't see any other cars so, maybe they're not booked out." She smiles at me with hopeful naivety. It takes me a beat to process what she is talking about.

"Oh, yes. Well, it was a hotel. And it probably will be again. But right now, it's closed."

"What? Oh, no. It's closed? I was hoping for a place to stay." Charlie's face is panicked. "This is terrible." She starts pacing. "Where am I going to sleep?"

"Don't worry. Um. Look. It's not ideal, I know," I say keeping my voice calm and even. "But you can stay here tonight."

Charlie looks straight at me, breathing heavily. "Are you sure? I mean…" She begins pacing again. "Maybe there's someone at the hotel who could let me in and…"

"There's no one there."

"But you're the caretaker? Security guard? Gardener?"

"Charlie. I own this place."

"Oh." Charlie laughs and shakes her head. "There I was thinking you were the gatekeeper or whatever. Ha. Funny me." She flops down on the couch still laughing and shaking her head, forgetting about her wet track pants, but clutching the dry ones to her chest. "I could have been in serious trouble there. If you hadn't come to my rescue, I would be dead. Frozen solid in my car for Christmas. Oh my. That's awful."

"Charlie. It's fine. You're safe here. Don't worry about anything. If you need something, just say. Um, otherwise, you should put on those dry pants."

Charlie doesn't seem to be listening. "Jason."

"Yup."

"You saved my life."

"All in a day's work ma'am." I head out to my room and shout back, "I'm going to take a shower. But please... make yourself at home." I grab a change of clothes and a fresh towel from the closet. "I don't have much but, you know, it's for sharing."

"Jason." Charlie's voice is small and timid. I see her from my room standing in the middle of the lounge, looking tiny in the multiple layers of my clothes. I pause in the doorway. "I don't know what I would have done, if you weren't here. It's kind of hit me..." Her eyes are wide. "It could have been very very bad."

"Yes. But it's not." I lean against the doorframe with the towel around my neck. "Charlie. You are fine. I am fine. The storm is going to blow through and then..." I try to assure my accidental guest. "Well, we'll figure it out."

"Yeah."

I turn to leave, then Charlie says, "Jason."

"Yes."

"Thank you."

"You're welcome. Charlie." The enormity of the situation has obviously just hit. I imagine Charlie is feeling suddenly vulnerable and helpless. It happens to people who experience trauma. The best thing to do is to offer some distraction. So, I say, "Hey, maybe check your phone. It'll be dry enough to plug into the charger now." She moves toward the arm of the chair and lifts her phone, then smiles at me, then looks across at the charger plugged into the wall socket.

"Yep. I'll do that."

Chapter 8

Charlie

"Listen, Charlie. I've been trying to call you," Lou's voice is strained and high-pitched on the line. "On your phone and that other number. The hotel guy. What's his name?"

"Jason."

"Yes. Jason. Anyway. So, Charlie. I can't come for you. I'm so sorry." She's trying to keep anxiety in check. "Emergency services are telling everyone, *do not drive anywhere.*"

"I know. I heard it on the radio. It's pretty bad." The wind is howling outside and I'm still in shock at the idea that I could be out there, stuck at the side of the road in my broken car; or walking to the highway in my impractical outfit; or frozen solid like a popsicle. I shiver, although I'm toasty warm, with my feet tucked under me, on the couch.

"They're telling people to stay put. Don't go out. It's a blizzard. Code R.E.D." There's a brief pause then she says, "Are you okay? Are you safe?"

"Reasonably." I hear the shower turn on in the bathroom.

"What does that mean? Reasonably."

"I'm just joking. I'm fine. Gosh. Actually, I'm more than fine." I snuggle into the warm cozy couch beside the roaring wood stove.

"I don't think this is the time for jokes, Charlie. I'm really worried."

"Don't be. I've been rescued."

"What? Where are you?"

"You know that birthday party we did in the summertime. August, I think. Isabel was the little girl's name. In the big house near the golf course."

"Yes. But..."

"You know when we left, there was that drop-dead-gorgeous dad who turned up as we were leaving. Looked a bit like Chris Hemsworth mixed with Austin Butler. Kind of moody; sexy; brooding."

"Oh yes. Who could forget him?" Lou's voice relaxes into her usual tone. "Although I thought he was more like a young Harrison Ford. Or, or, or, who's that guy in the TV show *Lucifer*?"

"Oh no. Not that guy. Too smooth."

"But handsome."

"Definitely handsome. But Jason is more like Chris Pratt in the *Jurassics*. All rugged and capable."

"Yeah. I see what you mean there. Anyway. We're off-topic. The dad at Isabel's party? What about him?"

"Well, he's not a dad."

"Charlie. What are you talking about? You've lost me. And why are you talking about a guy we saw at a kid's party months ago?" Lou shows signs of exasperation.

My voice drops to a hiss. "Because I'm in his house."

"What?"

"Lou. He's Jason, the hotel guy. I borrowed his phone to call you when mine was too wet to plug in."

"Okay. Go on."

"He, Jason, rescued me. He tried to jump-start Bertie, then when that didn't work, he towed me back to the hotel. And I thought, oh great, I'll just check into a room at the hotel, because, you know, it's a hotel. But it's closed."

"Oh, no."

"But, it's alright, because Jason owns the hotel."

"Yay. So, he can let you in and you can stay in a room?"

"Well, no. Because it's shut and there's no one there. Like no one."

"So, if you're not in the hotel, then where are you?"

"In the gatehouse, where Jason lives with Rocko, his dog, which is tiny. The house, not the dog. Rocko is enormous. One bedroom, a lounge, a kitchen, and a bathroom." I breathe and listen as the shower turns off. "Lou. I think I'm in love."

"Are you really?"

"Yes."

"But Charlie. Look. I don't want to catastrophize, but maybe he's an ax murderer."

"He's not."

"How can you be so sure?" Lou's voice is panicky again. "Wait there. I'm coming to get you, right now."

"No. Lou. You can't. Roads are closed and we've been told to stay put, remember?"

"Yeah. I know. But I'm scared for you."

"Lou. I'm okay." I can see how my situation looks from the outside. If it was Lou in my spot right now, I would want to come get her too. "Listen. I wasn't convinced, because you hear this sort of thing on... What's that TV show, *Don't Be a Dumbass*, something like that. And I've seen *Psycho*. I know what happens. But I spoke to his sister." Rocko ambles over, climbs up onto the couch beside me, and rests his big old head on my lap. "Lou. He's about the nicest person ever. Okay, so he's given me a lecture about road safety and what to pack to get yourself out of trouble on a trip. And he's a bit judgy about fairies and Christmas and whatnot. But that's because he's never been to Coachella."

"The hot guy from the party, huh? Wow. You're going to be snowed in with him?"

"Yes."

"Charlie."

"Yes?"

"Be careful."

"I am. And Rocko is a very cool dog. He is really big. About the biggest dog I've ever seen. But I think he likes me."

"Charlie. I'm so pleased you're safe. Thanks for calling me back. I was out of my mind with worry." There's a pause and I hear Lou talk with someone. "Calvin says hi. And if anything happens… Gosh. We're both going to come out there and…"

"Alright. I got to go." Jason opens the bathroom door and closes it behind him. "Lou. I love you."

"You too. Muah!"

Jason pauses in the living room doorway as he towels his hair. "Lou. Is that your boyfriend?" He smiles then walks through to the bedroom. "I have a bunch of missed calls from him on my phone."

"No. Lou. Louise. She's my best buddy," I say stroking Rocko's ears as Jason comes into the living room and sits on the wingback chair. "And also, my business partner. Well. There are three of us at Sparkle Entertainers. Lou's boyfriend, Calvin, is the third partner. He's a wizard."

The storm has fully set in and rages outside. Jason relaxes back and appraises me across the room.

"A wizard, huh?"

"Yes." I sit up tall. "I can sense that you're skeptical about the world of magic and wizardry, but I can assure you it is very much alive and real... in certain realms."

"Realms, huh?"

"I think you may have been deprived as a child and missed out on a little fairy magic." I tuck my feet under Rocko's warm furry body.

"You could be right." Jason carefully opens the stove door with the tongs and tosses in a log. Then he settles back into the chair. "It's going to be a long night." Jason sighs. "We don't have TV, so, please, tell me how you got to be a fairy. Is it a calling, like being a doctor or a teacher?

Did you get picked out from a lineup? How does it work, Charlie? Enlighten me. Please do."

"I'm not sure that you are in the right frame of mind to be enlightened."

"Oh yeah?"

"You're very closed off, Jason."

"I am?"

"Uh-huh. If I'm going to share my fairy journey with you, I need to feel that you are not sitting there belittling me and having a laugh at my expense. We may be snowed in together and I fully appreciate you rescuing me, but if I am purely entertainment for you, I will need to charge by the hour."

"Oh. Alright then."

"If, however, you are genuinely interested in me, what I do, and my passion. Then, that is different."

"Got it."

"Are you sure?"

Jason laughs. "Yes. Charlie… And you're right. I approached the getting-to-know-you conversation in the wrong way. I apologize. Should we start over, do you think?"

"Yes. That's a good idea. How about you leave the room and come in again."

"You want me to leave the room and come in again?"

"That's right. But with a better attitude."

"A better attitude?"

"Exactly. If you go out there…" I nod toward the bedroom. "…give yourself a shake, you know, to shake off your negativity, then come back in, and we'll start over."

Jason stands and walks out to the corridor. After a beat, he comes back and sits down on the chair again. He's smiling.

"I can't quite believe that I just did that."

"But do you feel less negative?"

"I'm going to say yes to that, Charlie." Jason settles back into the chair. "So, you're a professional fairy. That's unusual. I've never met a fairy before. Tell me. How did you get into it?"

"Well, Jason. Thanks for asking. When I was at design school, my friend, Lou, dressed up as a fairy for her niece's birthday party. She did such a good job that all the parents who were there, booked her to entertain at their kids' parties. Maybe you don't know, but parents talk, and word gets around. Pretty soon, she was getting booked out left and right. And she asked me if I wanted to join in with some of the parties. So, I had this fun side hustle that was paying for my studies, and one day, I said to Lou, why don't we make this our business? We did the math and made a website. That's when Lou met Calvin. And we started booking other entertainers and branched out into festivals and parades and even corporate events. Sky's the limit. I'm mostly doing admin and marketing now, but the run-up to Christmas is our super busy time, so I'll pull on my wings and get the glitter out."

"I had no idea."

"Yeah. We are doing very well. And overall customer satisfaction feedback is a four-point-eight, out of five, average."

"Well, that is interesting."

"Thanks. I think so."

"And you didn't finish your design degree?"

"No... But I could. If I wanted to." We're quiet for a few minutes both watching the firelight. "And what about you?"

"Oh, I never had wings. Or glitter." Jason stretches out his legs.

"I think you would look good with a little sparkle here and there."

Jason looks at me and laughs. "Oh, man. Maddie would love that. She's always trying to get me to dress up."

"And you don't? Dress up, I mean." I smile at Jason who shakes his head.

Jason sighs as if he's trying to picture himself in wings and glitter. "I suppose we should allocate sleeping quarters."

"Jason."

"Yes."

"Were you in the military?"

"Yes. How did you know?"

"Allocate sleeping quarters."

Jason smiles. "I forget, sometimes, that I'm not in uniform anymore." Jason stares at an unfocused point on the far wall.

"So, you quit?" I blurt out. I'm intrigued. I want to know all about my enigmatic, handsome host.

"Did I quit?" Jason says slowly. Then he follows with an upbeat, "No. I served out my contract and now I'm a respectable, upstanding, tax-paying civilian."

"With a hotel."

"Ah yes." Jason sighs. "It's temporary. I'm getting it ready for sale."

"You want to sell it?" I'm incredulous.

"Look. It was an inheritance from a distant relative who I never even met." He glances at the ceiling. "I know what you're thinking. How nice to get gifted a hotel. But it's actually costing me and..." He reaches his hands above his head and clasps his fingers together. "I just want rid of it. But nothing is happening before Christmas. All sales agents and lawyers are closed up for the holidays. So, here I am. With a hotel I don't want, for six weeks, at least."

"Oh. That seems…"

"What?"

"Oh no. It's not my business to say."

"I know what you're going to say. Because I had the same conversation with Meredith. Why don't I find out about the people who owned it? Why don't I take an interest in the history of the place? I could do something amazing. Bring it back to life." Jason snorts a laugh. "I've heard it all." He drums his fingers on the arm of the chair. "I'm just not… I'm not that person."

"So, you're going to sell it and… What happens after that?"

"Man, you're nosy."

"Sorry. Yes, I am." My hand reaches down to Rocko's head. "But, you know, we have all night. There's no TV. So, we can talk about all sorts of things. Dreams. Wishes. Ideas. Whatever you want." I shrug. "We can even make up stories. Doesn't have to be real or serious…"

Jason smirks across at me. I get the sense that there's something stopping him from just relaxing. He's so uptight. If we weren't snowed in together, would I be so intrigued? If he wasn't so attractive, would I be bothered trying to get through his obvious barriers?

"So, who were they, these people who built the hotel and lived here?" I ask gently.

"A great aunt on my father's side. Great Aunt Alice. That's her in the photo there." Jason points to a framed black and white picture of a young woman in an elegant evening gown, possibly taken in the fifties. She is styled like a Hollywood actress: Ava Gardner or Ingrid Bergman. High cheekbones. Harsh dark makeup.

"She's gorgeous. Was she famous?"

"I don't know."

"And you don't want to know?"

"That's right."

"Well. I want to know."

"Why doesn't that surprise me?" Jason laughs and our eyes meet in the warm cozy room. He holds my gaze for a brief moment of connection, then I sense his defensive walls again. His look says, leave me alone. But then. There's something else. Something softer, more vulnerable behind the tough manly exterior. I'm the first to look away.

"So, how come you called your dog Rocko?" I feel the need to lighten the mood.

"I had a roommate like Rocko one time. Lenny. A big old friendly, ridiculously generous guy with absolutely no sense of personal space. He was a dead ringer for Dwayne 'The Rock' Johnson. And when I called him out on his stuff that he'd leave all over the place, on the floors or furniture, I swear, he'd look at me with the same expression as Rocko – mildly surprised and a little bit hurt, but ever so apologetic."

We're quiet for little while, then I say, "Jason. I'm pretty tired after all the drama today. So, um, I was wondering about the sleeping arrangements."

"Of course. Yes. Sleeping arrangements. Well. You have my room. And I'll grab the couch with Rocko."

"Are you sure? I don't mind sleeping on the couch. It looks comfy and..."

"No. Please. You're my guest. I'd feel better if you had my room."

"Well. In that case. Thank you. Again. For everything."

Jason shows me to the tiny bedroom. It's only just big enough for the double bed and a set of drawers.

"The sheets were clean yesterday. I don't have another set, sorry."

"That's okay. It's five hundred percent better, a thousand percent better than sleeping in my car."

Jason steps past me to the set of drawers, pulls open the top drawer, and takes out a freshen-up pack with a fancy monogrammed logo on the side.

"I have a bunch of these. From the hotel," he says as he hands me the zip-up toiletries bag. "There's a toothbrush, toothpaste, some other lotions and stuff you might want. "I keep them handy, just in case."

"Just in case a fairy lands in your backyard."

"Something like that. Yes."

"Goodnight, Charlie. I hope you sleep well."

As Jason says these words the lights snap off and we're standing in inky blackness.

"Ooh. What happened?"

"Wait a minute," he says as he turns on his phone creating a feint eerie blue light that's only just bright enough to illuminate his face. "The power's out. It could just be a fuse for this house or perhaps it's the whole neighborhood. I'll go check."

"I'm coming with you," I say grabbing Jason's arm and staying close as we walk back into the living room.

Rocko, sensing something's up has hopped down from the couch and wags his tail, expecting orders.

"Lie down, boy. We're alright." Jason pats Rocko's head reassuringly. "Wait here." It takes me a moment to realize that he's talking to me, and not the dog.

"Oh, okay." I sit obediently on the couch. But then, Jason could have been talking to Rocko who jumps up beside me.

Jason disappears into the kitchen again leaving Rocko and I snuggled together. I wrap my arms around Rocko's warm, muscular body which instantly soothes and calms me. He leans into me, and I stroke his head. We sit together listening to the sounds of the storm outside that seem amplified by the enveloping darkness, and the additional noises of Jason opening and closing drawers and closets in the kitchen.

Chapter 9

Jason

I had just said goodnight to Charlie when the lights go out. We're in total darkness until I turn on my phone.

Charlie holds onto me as we make our way back to the living room where Rocko, sensing something is up, is alert and ready for a command. I tell him to wait, then Charlie says, "Oh, okay," and sits on the couch. Rocko jumps up beside her.

"I know I have candles and a lighter in here somewhere," I say as I keep walking to the kitchen, shining my phone light ahead of me. I pull open one drawer and then another. "Ah, here they are on the counter where I left them."

I open the box, pull out a candle, and light it with the Zippo. Then I find a small plate. I drip some hot wax onto the plate, then push the candle onto it so that the candle stands up straight and doesn't fall over. The tiny flickering flame throws out its brave yellow glow that fills the kitchen. I take the plate with the candle, shielding it with my hand, into the living room and place it on the sideboard. I turn to Charlie who has her arms around Rocko.

"I'll have a look at the fuse box to see if anything's blown in there. I'll be right back." I head back into the kitchen and open the cupboard door where the fuse box is located.

"Okay, we'll be right here," Charlie calls after me.

The fuse box is old, but the switches are all in the 'on' position. Everything looks okay. I turn off the main power then pull out each fuse to check. They look fine. I carefully put them back, but I don't turn on the mains in case of a power surge which would surely knock everything out when the electricity returns.

"Nah. It's nothing I can fix," I say, returning to the living room with another lit candle. "Must be a powerline down somewhere." The wind whistles down the chimney. Thumping and bumping, a tree thrashes its branches around, just outside the window. "I have more candles, but we don't know how long the blackout is going to last," I say putting the plate on the sideboard but blowing out the candle. Charlie listens. Her eyes are large dark shadows in the dimness. "So, we'll use them sparingly."

"Okay," Charlie says getting up to check her phone that's still plugged into the wall. She turns it on. "Oh, no. There's no reception. I have an error message." She holds it up for me to see. "*Try again later. Have a nice day.*" She laughs. "The storm must have knocked out the cell towers as well as the power." She puts down her phone on the sideboard. "But well done having candles. Were you planning a romantic evening? With Rocko or... "

"Nope. It's just best to be prepared." I sit on the other side of the couch next to Rocko who takes up most of the space in the middle. "Especially when you're out of the way. In a place like this with ancient wiring." A snort of laughter. "And ancient everything else." I pat my dog's head.

"Sounds to me like you've been in this situation before." Charlie resumes her position on the other side of my dog. She pulls up her feet and faces me. Rocko lies down between us and yawns.

"Not exactly. But military training and time in the forces makes you…" I take a deep breath. "It hardwires your brain to survive in any environment."

"Wow. I'm glad you're on my team." Charlie wraps her arms around her knees. "So, where were you stationed? Is that right? Stationed?"

"Yes. You can ask that. But if I tell you, I might need to kill you."

"Ha! Really?"

"No. Just jokes." I reach down to stroke Rocko's velvety ears. He sighs and smiles with his tongue out. "I was stationed in a few places."

"That's not descriptive or helpful at all."

"No. You're right."

"Okay. Let's try this one." Charlie sits up and looks at me directly. "Where was the last place you wore a military uniform? When was that?"

I'm quiet for a minute, then I say, "Kabul. Afghanistan. The airlift out after the Taliban takeover."

"You were there?"

"Yup."

"That must have been insane!"

"On one level. Yes. There's no denying the madness in a situation as complex as what was going on there, but… we, the servicemen and women, when we're called in to do a job, well, we just go ahead and do it..." I shrug and ruffle Rocko's ears as a distraction. "It's hard to explain."

"You must have seen some..." Charlie pauses. She breathes out. Then she says, "Jason, you're a hero." She shakes her head. "I couldn't be somewhere so chaotic. So violent."

"Yeah. Peacekeeping in a hostile place isn't for everyone. That's for sure." I smile and flick a sideways glance at Charlie. "I'm not a hero. I was one of many who were there because it's what we do. It's tough. No question about that, but I wouldn't trade the experience for anything."

"So, now you have all these military survival skills to use on your derelict hotel."

"That's right. And as you can see, Charlie. I'm putting them to good use tonight."

We laugh quietly in the warmth of the living room with a giant dog between us: I'm stroking Rocko's ears and Charlie's feet are wedged under his big furry body.

"I'm going to take a candle and go to bed now, if that's alright," Charlie says slowly extracting her feet, one by one, from beneath the sleeping dog.

"Okay. Well, take the Zippo and careful with the flame. The last thing we need tonight is a housefire."

"Got it." Charlie salutes, then picks up one of the plates with a candle on it. "Good night... Again."

"Goodnight, Charlie. Sleep well."

It's been a while since I've thought about Afghanistan. Sometimes the past is almost as clear and real as the present. Sometimes my military experience feels as if it belongs to someone else; as if I'm watching a newsreel on TV or something. Sometimes the sights, sounds, and smells of the Kabul evacuation crowd in on me. The airlift out, on one level, feels like such a waste. I guess I'm still processing what went on there. Of course, our units on the ground only knew what we needed to know. Our job was to carry out orders with efficiency and discipline. To keep people safe. To protect the vulnerable. To do our job. It was only afterward that I got a sense of the bigger picture.

Adjusting to a normal civilian life is tricky to navigate sometimes. I approach each day with a personal assessment of vital statistics, pulse, and heart rate: a monitor of well-being on an app on my wrist. It's comforting to see that physically everything is A-OK. I get a green check mark on a screen. And somehow it matters. It helps. It means I'm alive. A normal functioning human being. I can relax… a little bit.

I tap the screen on my wrist device and look at Rocko who has rolled onto his back, stretching out to occupy the whole couch. I'm wedged into one corner. His head shoves me further against the armrest as if I'm taking up too much space on my own furniture.

"Alright, boy?" I stroke Rocko's enormous head.

I much prefer sharing my space with a dog. In fact, I prefer animals over people any day. Life is generally easier. You don't need to explain yourself. There's no discussion. I'm free to do my own thing any time I choose. And Rocko, he's just happy going along with whatever I want.

Then, phew! Rocko has relaxed a little too much in the posterior area and, bam, the smell hits me full in the chest. I cover my nose and mouth and retreat to the kitchen to find a can of air freshener.

Good old Rocko, huh? I wonder if the smell has woken Charlie. I hope not. She might think it's me with the smelly bowel issue. Not the kind of impression I'd like my guest to have.

My mind drifts to thoughts of Charlie. The way she shivered at the gate. Her makeup streaked down her face. The pathetic inside-out umbrella. Such a sorry state. Something about her reminded me of a baby bird that has fallen out of its nest. I wanted to scoop her up and keep her warm and safe. How could anyone trail so much glitter? I'm still seeing it twinkle everywhere in the candlelight. She's only been in my house a few hours and I feel as if she has fully taken over.

But somehow, I can't be annoyed. I want to be, but Charlie looked so adorable swamped in my sweatshirt and track pants. Even without her wings and glitter, she looks like a fairy. If fairies were real, that is. I like her hair. And her cute smile.

I don't know why I'm thinking about my house guest when I'm searching for air freshener in the kitchen. Would I be having the same thoughts if she was a guy? Lenny, for example.

Eventually, I locate the can of air freshener in a bucket under the sink. I didn't buy it. Meredith did. She said it was for her and Maddie when they come to visit. I allowed her to put it in my kitchen. But there's no way I'm ever going to admit to using it.

This thought makes me laugh. I spray the can of floral essence in the air as I wander back into the living room. Then, I hear Charlie shout out. Rocko isn't on the couch. He isn't even in the room. I think I can guess what has happened.

Chapter 10

Charlie

The bed is super comfy, although it dips in the middle the way old beds do. I'm snuggled under a heap of blankets still wearing all Jason's clothes as it's a good bit colder in the bedroom than the living room.

And Jason. I could tell that he didn't really want me to stay in his house tonight. But he has a good heart underneath that gruff, tough exterior. He's not used to sharing. Anything. At all. Ever. He's used to having his own space without a glittery entertainer messing up the place. But I think, as we are stuck together in this predicament, he is resigned to the fact that he just has to put up with me. And I'll just try and be useful, and not get in his way.

It's a good thing I have Rocko to cuddle. At least the dog seems to like me.

And so, with thoughts of firelight, my feet all toasty under a big furry dog, and Jason's handsome face, all brooding and complex, my snooze turns into sleep. My final image is of Jason's eyes meeting mine in the soft orange glow. They seem to plead, *leave me alone*, but then, there's something else that says, *I'm not as tough as I make out. Please don't hurt me.* The candlelight showed something sad in his eyes. His tough rugged bone structure was sculpted beautifully in soft amber. When he turned toward me, I could tell there were a million thoughts that wanted to crash out, but he slowly shook his head and looked away. I guess there are some things he can't let go of yet. At least not with me.

I drift off to sleep to the sounds of the storm outside. I'm so grateful to be here. Safe. Warm. My situation could have been so much worse. I don't even want to think about that.

I'm not sure how long I slept but suddenly I'm awake. Eyes wide and all my senses on high alert. For a second, I don't know where I am, and it takes a couple of beats before the drama of the previous day allows me to make sense of my shadowy surroundings. The storm is still thrashing around and whistling about the house. But it's not these sounds that wake me.

In the darkness, I poke my head over the blankets and peer at the door. Even in the pitch black, I can make out the shape of the doorframe and detect motion as the door slowly swings open. I hold my breath for a moment and listen as footsteps approach the bed. There's someone in my room, breathing heavily with raspy inhalations.

"Jason?" I call out pretending to be brave. "Is that you?"

I pull the blankets up over my head as if they have the power to shield me from the maleficent presence close to my face. Then, I shake off my bleariness and suddenly remember where I am.

"Rocko. You devil," I say, laughing at myself and how my imagination had run away in my semi-sleepy befuddled brain.

Rocko's nose snuffles my face across the pillow. Then I hear him lick his chops before he bounds up, uninvited, onto the bed beside me.

"Well, hello fella. I'm not sure you're supposed to be in here." I pat the big dog's head.

At that moment, there's a knock on the open bedroom door.

"Oh, sorry about Rocko," Jason says from the doorway. "He thinks it's bedtime and, um, this is where he usually sleeps. I hope he didn't scare you."

I reach out for the Zippo, flick a flame, and light the candle. I squint to focus in the dim wavering glow.

"I was asleep and then, you know how your mind plays tricks on you when you're not fully conscious." I laugh. "I thought it was you."

"Me?"

"Yes. Heavy breathing. Bad smell."

"Oh. Thanks." There's a moment before Jason says, "Come on, Rocko. We're sleeping on the couch tonight."

Rocko lifts his head and looks at Jason as if he's a stranger who hasn't yet been introduced. Then, he lowers his head back to the comfy spot next to me on the blanket with a luxuriant sigh.

"Gosh. He's so perfectly well trained, isn't he?"

"I'll try that again," says Jason. He claps his hands and whistles. "Rocko. Hey buddy. Let's go. Quick... Now would be good. Alright. All in your own time." The dog doesn't move. Rocko has closed his eyes as if to block out the annoyance of a person trying to tell him what to do. "When you're ready. Okay... one, two, three... Go!"

This performance is hilarious. I'm trying to suppress giggles, but they bubble out of my mouth and cause the bed to wobble. Jason reaches for Rocko's collar and tries to lead him off the bed.

"You are in so much trouble and if there wasn't a storm, I'd throw you out right now," Jason says to his beloved hound. Then he turns to me and says, "He's not usually like this. I think he's showing off to get attention."

"Look. If he wants to sleep on the bed, you know, that's fine with me," I smile up at Jason who sits down and ruffles Rocko's ears. "I mean, who's to say that he won't try it again, right?"

"That's true. He's smart and he knows how to open doors. I mean, short of taking off the door handles, what else can I do? He can let himself in any time."

Rocko lifts his head again as if he's telling us off for making too much noise.

"Come on, buddy. Time's up," Jason says more direct and firmer this time.

Rocko thinks for a bit then heaves his bulk up to a standing position, gives himself a quick shake, then hops off the bed and out of the bedroom.

"Good boy… eventually," I say smiling at Jason.

"I'll put a chair in front of the door," Jason says standing to leave. "That should keep him out."

"Alright." I sit up and hug my knees up to my chest. "Are you going to be okay on the couch?"

"Yep. I'll be fine." Jason moves toward the door. "I'll try to persuade Rocko to sleep on the floor." He laughs. "I'm not sure how successful that's going to be." Jason pauses in the doorway and prepares to pull the door shut behind him. "Let's see if we can get some sleep now."

"Yeah. Goodnight Jason."

"Goodnight, Charlie."

I blow out the candle and wriggle back down under the blankets listening to the storm but thinking about Jason.

Chapter 11

Jason

Back on the couch, I'm not sleepy at all. Rocko has jumped up beside me and is turning around in circles before curling up to snooze again. I reach over to the stove, pick up the tongs and open the door, then toss in a couple of logs. Sparks rush around in a flurry when I poke the orange embers.

There's something deeply satisfying about poking a fire. Maybe that's what cavemen did. Sometimes I feel like a caveman, sitting in his cave with his big old obedient hunting dog. Except that, my big old dog is far from obedient. And tonight, he showed up my lack of dog skills, alright. But I wasn't really trying, and he knew it. Good boy.

The newly stoked fire burns brightly, and I'm cheered by the warmth. Is it just the fire? Or is it my house guest that has placed a contented glow somewhere in my chest. And just now, I didn't want to leave her. Not that I wanted anything to happen physically at all. Not that she isn't cute and attractive and…

I reach out and pat Rocko.

"You feel it too, huh?" I say to my doggie best friend.

Since Charlie entered my space, I just want to be around her. My attention switches to a sprinkle of pink glitter that's sparkling on the back of my hand.

"Has she put a spell on me, bud?"

My gaze turns to the fire again and think about the following day. Maybe the storm will blow itself out tonight, and I'll get Charlie's car going. Or I'll tow her to her house. Or maybe the storm will keep going and we'll be here, stuck together, for a week or more. How do I feel about that scenario? Pretty good, as it happens. I don't think that would be a bad thing at all.

"What do you think, Rocko? Would you be happy if Charlie stayed for a few days more?" Rocko is snoring happily. "Yep. Thought so. You like her. I can tell." I watch the flames consume the firewood. "Me too."

"Awww. It's so cool how you talk to Rocko. I'm sure he understands everything you say. He's a very smart dog."

I swing around to face Charlie. She's standing in the doorway wrapped in a blanket. Did she overhear me say out loud how I feel about her? I don't want her to know. I'm embarrassed and annoyed.

"Do you always sneak up on people?" I say, gruffly, hoping she'll just go back to bed and leave me alone.

"Not sneaking. No." Charlie shuffles into the room. "I'm going to get a glass of water. Do you want one?" She dumps the blanket on the couch.

"Sure. Thanks." I clench my jaw but resume politeness. "That would be good."

Charlie disappears into the kitchen and soon reemerges with a glass of water in each hand. She walks over to me and gives me one of the glasses.

"Thanks."

She sits next to Rocko on the couch and pulls up her feet, like she did earlier, then fixes me with her twinkly blue eyes. "I like you too, by the way."

I'm still embarrassed and defensive. "You don't even know me."

"Alright. I like what I know so far. And besides. Yesterday wasn't the first time I'd seen you."

"No? Sorry. Have we met before?" I set my expression to what I hope is 'mild surprise' and cross my fingers that my face doesn't betray me. I'm doing my best to protect myself. I don't want to admit to seeing Charlie before. That would give too much away. And I can't allow that. "I'm sure I would've remembered a fairy covered in pink glitter."

"Well, we didn't actually meet. But, I was an entertainer at Maddie's friend's party. Isabel, I think her name is... Does that ring any bells?"

"Tinkerbells?"

"Ha! You're so funny."

"Yes. Maddie reminded me." I sigh and look into the fire to hide my lie. "She told me when we saw you stranded at the side of the road. She said, 'Hey, there's Charlie the fairy.' Or something like that. But I don't remember seeing you at the party. I think I got there at the end. I was on uncle duty and stopped by to pick Maddie up."

"So. Yes. I have to admit that I was driving away with Lou, my friend, as you pulled up. And she mentioned something about your nice... car. Yes. That's what she mentioned."

"My nice car, huh?"

"Yes. And I looked over and saw you get out of your nice car." Charlie smiles awkwardly. "I know how lame that sounds." She laughs. "But I just wanted to let you know that it's because of Maddie that I feel comfortable here."

"Okay."

"I mean, you get a green light because you're a caring uncle and owner of a massive smelly dog."

"I had no idea the kudos attached to small children and large smelly dogs."

"Oh yes. You might have a glowing resume, but it means nothing but a string of words on a page. If I see how you are with kids and animals, well, that speaks volumes about who you really are. As a person who can be trusted... or not." She fixes me with an impish grin.

Charlie sits quietly for a while stroking Rocko. She sips her water. The fire crackles happily and we're quiet for a moment. In fact, everything is quiet.

"Hey," says Charlie. "The storm. Listen. I think it's gone. For now, at least."

"I think you're right. Let's hope so."

I drink some water, then put my glass down on the table beside me. Then I move down to the floor, stretch out my legs, and relax my back against the couch. Rocko snores peacefully.

I must have dozed off because when I wake up, it's morning. I'm covered with a jacket on the floor in front of the fire. Charlie is curled up under a blanket on the couch. And Rocko is nowhere to be seen. But I think I can guess where he is.

I open the stove and, quietly as possible, I place a couple of logs on the glowing embers, then close the door which squeaks on its hinges. The logs take a minute before they burst into flame. I watch with satisfaction as they begin to roar.

Charlie stirs but I don't think I woke her. I stand and walk to the bedroom as quietly as possible. And there, sure enough, is Rocko stretched out diagonally on the bed with a ridiculously happy face.

"Good morning, you scallywag."

Rocko doesn't move his head but gently beats his tail on the bed cover in response to my greeting.

"Come on. Your bladder must be fit to burst," I say at the bedroom door.

"Well, yes. You're right. Excuse me, please." It's Charlie. She stops and pokes her head in. "Look at that dog! Someone had a good sleep." She peers at Rocko and then at me with half-closed eyes, then shimmies past on her way to the bathroom. "Good morning, everyone."

"Good morning. How are you?"

"Sleepy," Charlie says from behind the closed bathroom door.

I haul Rocko off the bed and usher him to the front door. Luckily it opens inwards without a struggle, and I look out onto a magical wonderland of white sparkling snow. Rocko bounds out and leaps onto clean and even drifts where the driveway used to be. The cars are shapeless white mounds. I listen to the silence that is disturbed by a spatter and splat of dislodged snow that slides from a branch and onto the ground with a final plop. My breath billows and I rub my hands together to warm them.

Rocko is clearly delighted by the winter scene, so I leave him to roam around outside while I find my jacket and boots. The snow looks beautiful but all I see is a day of shoveling.

Chapter 12

Charlie

"It's so beautiful!" I squeal, barely containing my excitement, as I rush to the open door. "I can't wait to get out there and make snow angels."

"Wait a minute," Jason says, looking confused. "Don't you mean, 'I can't wait to get home'?" He checks his phone.

"Yeah. Yes, I do. But how many times do you get this kind of fabulous deep snow?"

"Too often." He scrolls down his screen not looking at me. "It's inconvenient and potentially dangerous."

"Ah, yes. You're right." My mind switches back to trudging down the road in the freezing sideways rain only the day before; the drama of being stranded at the roadside in my broken car; the relief of being rescued by a handsome, although reserved ex-army guy with all sorts of practical survival skills. "But I had a nice time last night." I beam enthusiastically. "It's been fun getting to know you, Jason. And Rocko."

Jason's eyes shyly flick up from the screen to meet mine. He clears his throat. "We have phone connection. The internet is back on and the weather looks good for the next couple of days. The storms moved on, and reports say, 'don't travel unless absolutely necessary. Emergency services and volunteers are clearing roads. Stay tuned for updates'."

"Well. That's super. We have time for snow angels. The conditions are just right. Come on."

"Um. Snow what?" Jason's brow is furrowed, his head on one side. "And, um." Jason breathes as if he's addressing a simpleton. "What exactly is a snow angel?"

"You're kidding, right?"

"No. No, I'm not."

"Well, come on. I'll show you." I take Jason's hand and lead him to the front door.

"Wait. If we're going outside, I think we need to dress appropriately, don't you?"

"Yes. You're right. I'll put my fairy dress back on." I say with seriousness. Jason stares hard at me but doesn't say anything. "Jeez. I'm joking! Jason. I am joking." I lean on the wall and indulge in some belly-holding mock laughter. "Yes. We should dress appropriately. Can I please borrow your coat again, and some boots?"

"Yes. Coat and boots coming up."

Jason reaches up and unhooks a thick padded oilskin coat. I climb into it and roll up the sleeves a bit. Then I pull on Jason's hiking boots and lace them up.

"They should be waterproof, but they're old so, don't complain if your feet get wet." Jason puts on a padded jacket and pulls on another pair of hiking boots.

"I'm not going to complain at all. This is going to be so much fun. You're going to love it."

We head out into the frosty air closing the door behind us, so the house stays warm. Rocko barks when he sees that we've come out to play as well. He jumps around unaffected by the cold.

"Is this Rocko's first experience of snow?" I ask.

"No. But he loves it. He's just like a puppy."

"Alright. Well, if you hold onto Rocko, just in case he wants to jump on me, I'll demonstrate." Jason holds onto Rocko's collar as I make my way to the flat area that is probably the front lawn of the hotel. "Now, as far as snow angel excellence goes, I don't believe there is a national certificate or anything formal. But I am the best. So, please. Watch and learn." I sit back in the middle of the crisp, crunchy snowy blanket, then lie down with my arms by my side. "This is the start position," I shout to the sky.

I have no idea if Jason is watching or listening but, simultaneously, I raise each arm, stretched away from my body, marking the snow, incrementally, until my arms are straight above my head. At the same time, I open and close my legs like a pair of scissors. When I'm confident I have created the most beautiful snow angel in history, I carefully roll up into a standing position, give myself a shake, then bow theatrically as if I have just won gold at the Olympics. I wave at the imaginary judges who have all given me a standing ovation and are holding up scorecards displaying straight 10s.

"Now it's your turn," I say with a big smile.

"You know what? I'll pass." Jason releases Rocko. "Thanks, though, for the informative demonstration. I'm going to get a shovel. Maybe I can dig us out of here today." He walks off. "And get you home."

My jovial mood falls flat. I look at my perfect snow angel and see how pathetic it is. Of course, we have more important things to do than playing in the wonderful, magical snow. I feel like crying although I'm not sure why.

"Pull yourself together," I mutter under my breath as I stomp behind Jason back into the tiny gatehouse. I shake off my childish silliness and bravely say, "Okay, partner. Tool me up."

Jason hands me a small spade from a stack of tools beside the door. He takes a big one.

"Here you go. I guess we'll start from the cars and make a trail to the gate. See how that goes."

"Gotcha, boss."

I don't know why, but I want to pummel Jason with snowballs and squish his face into my snow angel until he relents and promises to make one himself. But I don't. Although the image of Jason's stern expression squashed into a snowdrift does make me smile. Then I'm ashamed of my malicious thought. How could I even think of being mean to the man who saved my life? This thought makes me smile even more. And then, my smiles all disappear because I'm a little sad our time together is coming to an end.

The weak winter sunshine bounces off the dazzling snow. Rocko bounds around playfully billowing steamy breath.

I've cleared the snow from the cars. It slid off easily in satisfying chunks. I'm pleased with my progress and turn to see if Jason has noticed my excellent effort, but he's too busy clearing the snow from the driveway. I can't help but watch him. He's like a machine. He has taken off his jacket and attacks each shovelful with energy and physicality which is truly admirable. I'm breathless just watching his manly shoulders and arms flex with rhythmic effort. I feel redundant but I take off my jacket, hang it on the gate too, and get stuck into the job at hand with my little shovel.

After a few minutes of shoveling snow from the driveway, I'm exhausted. I stop for a breather and allow myself to be distracted by Rocko who has dropped a stick at my feet.

"You just want to play, huh?"

I pick up the stick and throw it as far as I can. Jason stops shoveling snow to watch. I smile at him, but he looks away and keeps shoveling. The bright sunshine is turning the white crispy snow to mush. I notice that my snow angel has all but disappeared.

"See." I point to the angel shape where dark grass is poking through. "It's too late for you to make your snow angel now."

"What?" Jason says, but he doesn't look up.

"Oh, nothing." I keep shoveling.

Chapter 13

Jason

I'm annoyed. The physical exertion of shoveling snow is helping but still, I'm annoyed. I'm annoyed at the snow. And irritated by Charlie. Well, that may be a little unfair. I'm just embarrassed because she overheard me telling Rocko that I like her. And it's true. I do like her. But there's no way I want her to know that. Not now, in the cold light of day, that shows up all our differences in stark contrast like snow on dark branches. She's all shiny and glittery and I'm all practical and serious. But last night, in the warmth of the fire and candlelight, I stupidly let my guard down. And that's why I'm annoyed. Somehow, she has broken through what I thought were my impenetrable defenses. And so easily. With her laugh, and her sparkly blue eyes, and her lips that I just want to kiss all the time. And with all that pink glitter that's still everywhere.

I scoop another shovelful of snow. The metal scrapes the asphalt sending juddering vibrations up my arms. I'm getting too warm in my jacket, so I take it off and hang it on the gate.

But mostly, I'm annoyed at myself. I mean, she only wanted me to join in her game. And I couldn't even do that. Yes. Making snow angels looked like fun. And, yes, part of me wanted to jump around in the snow like we're starring in our own cute Christmas romcom. But...

I stop shoveling and watch Charlie throw a stick for Rocko. She's so pretty. And alive. Watching her hopeless stick-throwing skills warms my heart and makes me laugh. What is happening to me?

For a minute, I picture us living here. Happily. Together. Where did that come from, soldier?

I shake the thought away and shovel some more snow that is turning to mush by the minute as the day warms up. And I remind myself that I'm a lone wolf. That's it. Me, myself, and I. And Rocko, of course. And, besides, there's no room for anyone else here in the gatehouse. We would end up tearing each other to pieces in such a small space.

Or we could be the happiest people in the world. I gulp. The shovel drops from my hand and clangs on the hard wet driveway.

Charlie looks over and laughs. Then she throws the stick for Rocko again.

I feel overwhelmed with blissful serenity. As if I want this moment to last. I want Charlie here with me. She makes everything beautiful. Even a life-threatening situation of being snowed in was kind of fun because of Charlie.

I give myself a shake, then pick up my shovel and survey the cleared path, banked up either side with gritty grey melting snow all the way to the gate. I snort clouds of steam like a dragon.

I don't want to be grumpy. But it's the only way I know how to be. Perhaps Charlie can teach me to lighten up. Maybe it starts with snow angels. But I guess I've missed that opportunity. I've missed a simple fun thing and now it's too late. I pause my shoveling again. What is wrong with me? Why do I think I need to change? I don't. But then... Suddenly I'm sad and anxious.

Charlie has got under my skin, alright. For the first time in a long time, I'm conflicted. I don't know what I want anymore. This is intense. I don't even know why. My guard has been up for so long I'm not even sure it can come down. Or if I want it to.

The driveway is clear to the gate. I pull the chain through. The gates creak as I pull them open. The snow on the road up ahead is melting, but I'm aware that as the sun goes down, the surface water will freeze over like a skating rink, making the drive to town impossible. I check my phone for road conditions and travel updates.

"If we're going, we'd better go now," I shout over to Charlie who is doing her best to run around in my hiking boots with Rocko in the winter sunshine. She stops running and turns around, combing hair out of her eyes with her fingers.

"Okay," she says looking back at me.

We stand still facing each other for a moment. I wonder if Charlie is thinking the same idea as me, that maybe I don't tow her back home today. We have enough food and firewood. And what if she stays for another night here with me? Maybe it will snow again, and I'll have another chance to make a snow angel on the front lawn. And I won't be so grumpy. And maybe I can tell her that I like her and that I remember seeing her at a kid's birthday party in the summertime. And how I thought she was pretty then. And that she's pretty now.

I'm hoping Charlie will say something like, 'Do I have to go? Can I stay here with you and Rocko?' But she doesn't. Charlie drops her gaze and walks to the gatehouse and out of sight.

Rocko gives me a look that says, "See what you've done, idiot? It's all your fault."

Chapter 14

Charlie

"How about you call him and stop moping around like a world-class moping around champion?" Lou says exasperation in every syllable. She flops down onto the couch next to me in our living room.

Festive lights pulse in multi-colored disco rhythms around the window looking out to the street. An illuminated snowman takes up position in the corner, opposite our enormous, over-decorated Christmas tree. I scan the chaotic loops of tinsel and all manner of ornamentation that are haphazardly crammed into our living room, from floor to ceiling, and think about Jason.

It's been a week since I was snowed in with the most beautiful man in the world and his big smelly dog, and I can't quite get back to normal. Whatever normal is. It's as if I left a part of myself in that little gatehouse, like an abandoned sock left under the bed.

"Call who?" I say back to my roommate.

After we cleared the snow from the driveway and shoveled it away from the gate so it would open, Jason hooked up my car and towed me to a garage in my neighborhood. It was slow going on the country back roads, wet with meltwater runoff and treacherous with fallout from the storm. We had to stop a couple of times to move large branches off the road so we could pass. The city streets were better, having been cleared, then scattered with grit, to stop the expected ice-rink freeze up. Thankfully, traffic was minimal. Sitting in Bertie's driver's seat, my foot covered the brakes, as we coasted into the outer suburbs, then to the car mechanic, who is familiar with my ancient rust bucket of a vehicle. Miraculously, the sign on the customer's door displays *Open*.

Jason stops in the parking lot and unhooks the tow rope. I pull on the hand brake, open the door, and get out. I'm nervous and I don't know what to say. Jason speaks first.

"We made it." He coils the rope around his hand and elbow. "I hope you can get him fixed. And it's not going to be too expensive." I nod. "It may even be worth looking around for a new car."

"A new old car?"

Jason laughs. "Yeah. A newer car in better working condition. Something reliable and road-worthy." I nod some more and try to think of something to say, but everything seems trite and clichéd. I open my mouth, then close it again. "You okay?" asks Jason.

"Yes. Sure. I'm fine. Everything's fine. And, Jason... thank you. Really, I... don't know what else to say, but... You saved my life. I'm not even being dramatic. Which is unlike me. I'm nearly always dramatic."

"Charlie." Jason interrupts my blathering. "You are welcome. I'm happy we got you back safely, so..." He extends his hand out for me to shake. Formal. Business-like. Impersonal.

"So... *hasta la vista, baby*?"

"Yes." Jason laughs and I feel my cheeks color up as I cringe at my inappropriate *Terminator* reference. "Take care, Charlie. Maybe I'll see you again."

Then Jason; love of my life; the most beautiful man in the world; my hero; my everything, takes a step back and gets into his Chevy. He starts the engine and drives away. And what do I do? Nothing. I just stand there, rooted to the spot, with a million astonishing thoughts on quick-fire, pinging around my brain.

I want to run after him and jump through his open window and cover him with kisses and tell him how I feel. But I don't do anything. I just stand there in the mechanic's parking lot and watch him go.

"Jase the Ace, of course. Charlie." Lou is still exasperated. "You are getting a medal for denial."

"I can't call him. I don't know what to say." I slump back into the cushions. "I'll just wait until he calls me."

"What? After you said, *hasta la vista, baby,* in your Arnold Schwarzenegger voice. He's never going to call you."

"No. you're right, Lou. I blew it. The *Terminator* reference was the kiss of death, wasn't it?"

"Yes." Lou sighs theatrically. "But stranger things have happened. And, from what you've told me about what happened up there at his place, I think he really likes you."

"It did seem that way. At the time. And that's what he said to his dog."

"Maybe he's waiting for an appropriate delay before he calls you, because he doesn't want to appear needy or desperate," my friend says encouragingly. "Or, maybe he's shy and waiting for you to call him."

"Maybe. But I don't want to appear needy or desperate either."

"No, you won't," says Lou, turning sideways to face me with a glint in her eye. "Because you are the rescuee who is super grateful and must contact the person who saved her life and give them a thank-you gift. Or something. Charlie." Lou thumps my leg. "And besides, then you'll know one way or the other if you imagined - now how did you put it? – 'Jason's soft searching look in the candlelight'."

"Oh, Lou." I clasp my hands to my face wanting to hide. "I feel such a dummy. There was no soft searching look. It was only the candlelight. I imagined the whole 'spark' thing." I'm agitated and stand up to pace up and down. "I tell you what. I'm going to drive over there. Like you said, I'll give Jason a thank-you gift and then we'll see what happens next. Maybe nothing. Maybe something."

"Great! That's great. And you'll stop moping around and being a big sad sack of sadness. Now, what are you going to get the man who saved your life?"

"Something amazing! Something he didn't know he needed. Something special that no one else would think to give him."

"A watch."

"He has a Fitbit." I keep pacing.

"Okay."

"A Harry Potter wizard wand. I'll order one online."

"No. It'll take too long to arrive."

"Yes, you're right." I pace some more and think. "Juggling balls."

"Does he juggle?"

"No. But I can teach him."

"Actually," Lou says tapping her fingers, thoughtfully, on her lips. "That might work."

"I know," I say still pacing. "I'll get Rocko a new collar. A Christmas collar for special occasions."

"That's a great idea. A gift for the dog. Brilliant."

Everything seemed rational and in place when I was discussing the gift with Lou. Even Calvin said it was a genius stroke when we ran the idea past him about a Christmas dog collar for Rocko. He assured me that, from a guy's perspective, it shows thoughtfulness without being over-the-top emotional or too personal.

Now I'm in the car, driving out to the closed-up Mansion Hotel, I'm rethinking my gift choices. I did get the juggling balls in the end after a great deal of deliberation. And I wrapped them up with a note saying that I could teach Jason to juggle any time he wants to learn.

So, there are two gifts on the seat beside me. And the bag of clothes that I borrowed from my life-saving hero. Jason said I could keep them, but it didn't seem right. However, I did enjoy sleeping in his t-shirt and I almost kept it. But then, I thought, what if he notices that all the items are there in the bag except one t-shirt? Then, I'd have had to think of something else to say that doesn't sound creepy or weird. Something other than the truth. *Yes, Jason. I kept that t-shirt because it smells of you. I hope you don't mind...*

As I approach the hotel gate my stomach twists and flutters with anticipation. I check myself. I've never been this jittery before. I park on the road outside the gate, and I take a deep breath before getting out of my newly-fixed car. Then, I see Rocko. He barks and wags his tail when he sees me. I grab the gifts and bag of clothes and walk over to where he is with his paws high up on the gate.

"Rocko! It's so great to see you." I reach in with my spare hand and ruffle his soft ears. "Where's your friend? Is he home or is my timing all off?"

Rocko nuzzles my hand and leans in for a pat through the wrought ironwork.

I look up the driveway. There's no sign of Jason's Chevy. I notice how different the place looks from how I remember it. There's no snow today. I know I shouldn't be sad about that, but Christmas is only two weeks away and it would be so nice to have that frosty festive feeling to go with my gifts.

I pull the chain through each side to let myself in, then pull the gate shut and replace the chain. Rocko trots along ahead of me to the gatehouse. I call out hello, then listen for a reply. I knock on the door and wait. Nothing.

I'm disappointed. I should have called to make sure Jason would be here. But then, perhaps it's better this way. I leave the bag of clothes on the shelf by the door and the wrapped up juggling balls in Christmas paper with a shiny satin ribbon, and the card that reads, *Merry Christmas. I hope all your dreams come true.* I wrote my number on the card too and said that Lou, Calvin and I would love to invite him for Christmas dinner, if he's available.

I unwrap Rocko's present and fasten the red tartan collar around his powerful neck. It was the biggest size in the store, and it fits perfectly. I snap off a sprig of holly with berries from a bush nearby and attach it to the brass buckle.

"Merry Christmas, Rocko. Don't you look handsome?"

Then, I have a brainwave. Jason may be in the hotel, fixing it up or whatever. Maybe the Chevy is parked around the back, out of sight.

Rocko pads along with me as I walk from the gatehouse to the hotel's front door. I cup my hands beside my head and peer in through the elegant etched windows surrounding the large, impressive door. A gust of wind blows brittle brown leaves in a swirl around my feet on the marble floor of the stone portico. Then I hear a child's laughter, so I walk around to the back of the house.

Chapter 15

Jason

It's been a week since I dropped Charlie off at the auto repair shop downtown. But somehow, she's still with me. It's ridiculous. And it's not just the pink glitter that refuses to be hoovered up. I miss her. It's hard to admit but it's true. I miss the way she curled up on the couch with her feet tucked under Rocko. I miss the way she said things; the way she got excited about the snow; the way she sang in the shower. She surprised me. She knocked me off guard. Sideways. She got to me.

I thought about calling her. I already have the number for Sparkle Entertainers from the call she made from my phone in the storm. So, why have I been delaying this mission? And why did I drive away from her so abruptly at the mechanic's? Because, let's be honest here, I was as scared as heck. I drove away fast because I didn't want to say goodbye. And I didn't want any kind of tug on my heart. But that's exactly what I'm feeling now. Tugging and nagging. The idea of calling Charlie is nagging me. And I'm getting nagged by Meredith and Maddie. I called round to see them after I dropped Charlie off. I was restless and didn't want to drive straight back to the mansion.

"What?" says Meredith, incredulously when I turn up unannounced. "You left her at a repair shop?"

"Yes, Meredith. Her car needs some serious work. I'm not sure if they'll have the parts for it. It may not be fixable at all."

"Stop. Stop. Stop." Meredith holds up her hands. "Did you at least get her number?"

"I have her work number and her friend's number." I hold up my phone. "She made the call from my phone because her phone wasn't charged up."

Maddie comes into the kitchen.

"Hey, Jason. I thought it was you. Where's fairy Charlie? You didn't bring her over with you?" Maddie's little hands plant firmly on her hips. She fixes me with an accusatory stare. "Why?"

"We're just discussing that, sweetie," says Meredith turning from her daughter back to me.

I'm about to defend myself with a lie. Something about Charlie wanting to get back to her friends, but I think better of it, not wanting to add fuel to the fire.

"I'm going now," is all I say. And I backtrack out of my sister's house, climb into the Chevy, and drive away.

I can see how the situation looks for Meredith and Maddie. And it doesn't put me in a good light. As I drive back up the hill carefully in the dark, I hope my tires have enough grip to stop me sliding out of control. I will call Charlie but I'll choose my moment and call when I am good and ready. And not because I'm being bullied into it. Maybe tomorrow. Or the next day. I don't want to come across as needy or desperate.

In the library of the closed-up Mansion Hotel, I laugh at myself as I grab a handful of books and stack them in the cardboard carton at my feet. I figure I'll get everything that's not nailed down in the hotel, boxed up ready for the valuation guy who's scheduled to come in the New

Year, sometime. Although I don't have firm dates yet. I've been keeping myself busy to avoid calling Charlie. But the longer I leave it, the harder the task becomes. I've been doing everything possible to fill up my days, but that isn't making things easier, the way that I'd hoped it would. The nagging, "Call Charlie," is on repeat in my head and, what began as a whisper, is now an unavoidable yell.

I pack the leatherbound titles carefully, spines facing up, as requested. Then, I pause my action to look around the elegant room and the empty bookshelves. My gaze falls on the stack of cardboard cartons, full of books that I've stacked against the wall. I could always burn them on the fire. It would probably make better economic sense to do that.

Maddie comes rushing in.

"Hey, Jason." She's dressed in her thick warm pink sweater with a string of pearls looped twice around her neck. She found them in a box of jewelry and was over the moon when I said she could keep them.

"Hey, Maddie." She's 'helping' me pack up the hotel's chattels. Meredith dropped her off and I'm taking her home later.

"Can I show you something?"
"Sure. What is it?"

I follow Maddie to the wide, open living room area overlooking the untamed garden.

"I'm not sure." Maddie takes me by the hand and leads me to a panel in the wall. "It's in a secret closet," she whispers with wonder. I didn't realize before, but there is a closet door. It has the appearance of the surrounding pale blue wall and blends in. "Look at this."

Maddie pulls open the secret closet which reveals an ornate inlaid wooden cabinet with decorative mirrors and gold details. In pride of place on top is an old-style gramophone, with a winding handle and huge brass trumpet, possibly from the twenties or thirties. Underneath the gramophone, a double set of glass doors displays two shelves of dog-eared record sleeves.

"What is it, Jason?" Maddie's eyes are wide with curiosity.

"It's a gramophone."

"A gramophone. It's so beautiful. What does it do?"

"It plays music."

Maddie's eyes almost pop out of her head and her mouth falls open. "Can I hear the music? Does it work?"

I sigh, as all plans to pack up the hotel would now be on hold until I got the ancient music machine working.

"Well, we can try, Maddie." My niece laughs, jumps up and down clapping her hands, which makes the pearls of her necklace click together joyously.

As I watch Maddie's exuberance, my attention is caught by someone peering in through the conservatory door. My heart leaps to my throat because I know who it is immediately. It's Charlie. She looks adorable in jeans, knee-high boots, a padded jacket, and a colorful knitted stripey beanie and scarf. A very different look from the sparkly fairy outfit she was wearing when we first met. She sees me, then steps back from the door and waves. A rush of happiness fills me as our eyes meet. The moment stops time. Then I snap into action and hurry to the door to let her in.

"Hey. Jason. I hope you don't mind me interrupting but..."

"Gosh. Charlie. I was just thinking about you."

"You were?"

"I mean. Yes." I cough nervously. "I was wondering if you got your car fixed."

Maddie runs over to join us. "Hey, fairy Charlie. What are you doing here? Do you like my necklace? Jason said I could keep it."

"Yes, I do. It's very pretty." Charlie crouches down to look at Maddie's necklace up close. "Do you know what the beads are?"

"Yes. They're pearls from the ocean and probably belonged to a mermaid." Maddie twirls with her arms out. "And now they belong to me." She stops twirling. "I hope the mermaid is okay with that."

"I'm sure she is."

"So, Charlie, welcome." I suddenly find my voice, and something to say to mask my delight at seeing her.

"Wow. So, this is the legendary Mansion Hotel." Charlie follows me into the living room and takes in the generous dimensions and architectural design. "It's gorgeous, isn't it?"

"A gorgeous albatross around my neck," I shake my head and snort a mirthless laugh.

"What's an alba-truck?"

"An albatross, Maddie, is heavy burden someone is forced to carry. Something they don't want that weighs them down."

Charlie glints a sideways smile at me. "It doesn't have to be," she says.

I exhale audibly. "Now, don't you start. We've already had that conversation."

"Hey, Charlie. We found a secret closet with a... what did you call it?"

"A gramophone."

"No way," says Charlie excitedly. "Can I see it? Does it work?"

"We can try."

Now I have two distractions leading me away from packing books and doing useful things and back to the gramophone in the secret closet. One on either side. I sneak a glance at Charlie who is smiling from ear to ear. I look away quickly hoping she doesn't notice, but not quickly enough. She catches me looking and wrinkles her pretty nose at me which causes an involuntary cough and my stomach to flip. Charlie stands in front of the gramophone, her eyes sparkling with excitement.

"It's beautiful. I don't think I've ever seen one of these before. Maybe in a museum. How extraordinary." Charlie reaches out to touch the musical artifact. "Jason, you are so lucky to have one in your house. Hotel, that is." Charlie beams at me and Maddie beams too. "Maddie," Charlie says. "Would you like to turn the handle?"

"Yes." Maddie's eyes gleam with anticipation.

"Alright." I step in barring Maddie from touching the ancient object. "Before that happens, I'm going to check that it's not hazardous in any way."

"What? Like explosives or a booby-trap," says Charlie, teasing.

"Actually, no. But these old things could be spring-loaded, and I wouldn't want Maddie to get hurt. I take uncle duty very seriously."

"He really does," says Maddie rolling her eyes as if my care and attention are things she must endure.

I check around the gramophone and test that nothing is about to fall off. I check the stylus, which looks secure and ready to go. I gently spin the turn table, which moves with surprising ease.

"Seems fine. Maddie. Would you be so kind as to wind the handle?"

Maddie nods graciously and I pick her up so she can reach.

"Wait a minute," says Charlie. "What are we going to listen to? What records do we have?"

"Ah. Good point." I put Maddie back down on her feet.

"And maybe..." Charlie is at my side. "Do you have something to clean it off first so dust doesn't ruin the record? A rag or a cloth. A tea towel, maybe?"

"Sure." I hurry to the reception desk in the hallway where I left a bucket of cleaning products, cloths, and sponges. When I come back, Charlie has pulled out one of the vinyl records from its sleeve. She studies the label.

"This is what people used to play music on before there was Spotify," she tells Maddie who is enthralled.

"No way."

"Yes." Charlie nods and smiles at the little girl. "This is extremely clever and you're going to love it." Charlie reads the label out loud. "Duke Ellington. He was famous. Right up there." She puts the record carefully back in its sleeve and repositions it on the shelf, then pulls out another disc in a tatty cover. "This one. Oh my." She puts a hand on her chest. "It's so great. Bing Crosby." Charlie looks with reverence at the faded label showing through a circular hole in the protective paper sleeve. "Do you know it? 'White Christmas'."

Charlie's eyes shine. I am mesmerized. How could I refuse her anything? She holds my gaze before Maddie says, "Are we going to play some music or just stand around staring at each other?"

I carefully use a damp cloth to wipe the surfaces free from dust. Then, Charlie slides the disc out of its sleeve and places it on the turn table. She steps aside as I lift Maddie up so she can turn the handle. But it's too stiff for Maddie to crank, so I ask Charlie to help out and put Maddie down on her feet.

Finally, Charlie cranks the handle four or five times.

"I hope it's not broken," she says.

"Nothing's happening," says Maddie with a perfect upside-down smile.

"Oh, what about taking the brake off?" Charlie says, reaching for a shiny metal bar close to the turn table. It clicks as she pushes it to the side and the record begins to spin.

"Ah," exclaims Maddie. "It's magic."

Charlie lowers the arm with the stylus onto the revolving disc. It crackles and hisses and then we hear the orchestral introduction.

The music sounds wobbly and there's a lot of interference but, somehow, the lack of clarity adds to the listening experience, and I feel as if I'm transported back in time.

There isn't enough power in the motor to finish playing the record and Bing Crosby's voice gets deeper and slower as the turn table slurs to a stop. Charlie carefully lifts the arm clear of the record.

"Well, thanks for that. It's a wonderful piece of history, isn't it?"

"Wonderful," says Maddie dreamily.

"And it doesn't need electricity to work," says Charlie. "You just wind the handle. It would've been great to have this in your house when we were stuck in the storm, Jason."

Memories of being snowed in with Charlie flood my mind, but they are quickly replaced with a deep longing to be snowed in with Charlie again. For longer this time. With a gramophone and a stack of old romantic 78s.

Chapter 16

Charlie

Maddie didn't seem surprised to see me at all. But the look on Jason's face when he spotted me through the window is something I'll remember forever. The warmth in his smile when his eyes met mine. Then, he was bashful and looked away. I could tell he was trying to be cool, but he was clearly flustered. In a good way.

Stepping in through the patio door of the old Mansion Hotel was pure magic. Just like stepping back in time. Dust sheets cover the furniture and pictures, but I get tingles at the grandeur of the place that hasn't changed in decades.

I can appreciate how Jason is overwhelmed by the task of getting it ready for sale. He doesn't want to be here and he's making it hard work for himself. But I sensed that when we got the gramophone going and played 'White Christmas', he relaxed and even seemed to enjoy getting the old machine working for his little niece. The moment felt like heaven.

Maddie runs off to play princesses and host a pretend tea party for some royalty who are stopping by, leaving Jason and me alone by the gramophone. I feel suddenly shy.

"So, Charlie. What brings you all the way out here today?" asks Jason with reserved politeness. "Is it purely a social call or are you interested in purchasing a grand old hotel that needs a whole lot of TLC?"

"Oh. Just a social call. And I dropped off a thank-you gift. For you and Rocko. I left it on the shelf at the gatehouse. I thought you weren't at home, then…"

"You came snooping."

"That's right. I did." I laugh. "I can't help it. I'm just nosy."

"I know." There's a pause then Jason says, "So, would you like a personal tour of the old Mansion Hotel?"

"Would I? I thought you'd never ask."

Jason shouts out to Maddie that he's showing me around. Maddie shouts back, okay, as I follow Jason out to the main hall and reception area.

"Here we are at the grand entrance. Before it was a hotel, it was my great, great grandfather's private residence." Jason's voice echoes as we begin to climb the sweeping marble staircase. "I've been doing a bit of digging since I saw you last. About the family. My ancestors. The people who built this place."

"Cool. I want to know everything."

"Well, Cedric Winston Archibald Clayton Harris made his fortune on the railroads. He was good friends with the Rockefellers who built one of their houses just down the road." We arrive on the landing where corridors lead off in opposite directions. Ghosts of pictures that have been removed still hang on the wallpaper "They played golf together and socialized in similar circles. You know, the movers and shakers of the time, I guess."

"Wow. That's so interesting." I follow Jason through an open door to a vast bedroom decorated with wallpaper covered in delicate birds and flowers. "This room is incredible." A massive bed with a carved gold headboard dominates the space and is positioned to take in the full-length windows down to the gardens below. Luxurious swags of pale green drapes frame the view.

"Yes. And the adjoining bathroom is pretty special too," Jason says walking toward a door in the far corner. I follow him through to where a huge white claw-footed bath sits in the middle of the room tiled in black and white ceramic designs.

"Now that's the bathroom I want someday."

"It's yours. It comes with the house if you want to buy a rundown monster of a place."

Jason shows me other rooms upstairs, then we take the servants' stairs down to the kitchen and scullery on the ground floor. I imagine the small army of staff that must have been needed to run this place and the difference between these people and the wealthy guests they were serving.

Jason opens a door, and we descend to the basement and wine cellar.

"I'll show you a photo of this wine cellar packed with bottles and barrels," says Jason. "It must have been quite the party house in its day."

"Yeah. I get that feeling."

I'm so pleased I came here today. All my nerves from the drive up here have evaporated as my nosiness takes over. Every room is a delight. And I feel privileged to be shown around this beautiful, yet rundown property. I wonder what will happen to it after it's sold.

"What other treasures are you finding?"

"Oh, it's mostly just junk." Jason smiles. "I think anything truly valuable was sold off to pay for heating bills years ago."

"It's great that you have time to be here, to get things organized. It's a massive job."

"Yeah. Well. I don't have a contract at the moment, so I said to Meredith that I'd do whatever is necessary to get this place on the market. Then, when it sells, we'll split the proceeds. And that will be that. And I'll be free to continue living my best life."

"And, excuse me for being nosy again, but what is that? Your best life."

"Another great question, Charlie." But Jason doesn't elaborate, he keeps walking. "All that's left to show you is the garage."

"Great."

We leave the house by the grand front door and disturb Rocko who is snoozing in a patch of sunshine on the portico step. He jumps up and wags his tail eagerly.

"Hey. What's that you're wearing, Rocko?" Jason is talking to his dog but he's looking at me with a crooked smile. "Looks like a new collar."

"Don't you think red plaid suits him?"

"Very stylish. And festive."

"It's my thank-you present. For rescuing me. In the storm."

"Well, there's really no need. We did what anyone would do." Jason pats the big dog's head. "Didn't we Rocko?"

"And bringing gifts gave me a valid excuse to come back here and be nosy."

"You are welcome. Any time." Jason smiles and looks into my eyes. I want to touch his hand which is a finger distance away from mine. "You don't need an excuse to come and be nosy." My fingers reach out. "Just... Any time." Jason gently takes my outstretched hand and holds it in his.

"Thanks."

Jason doesn't let go of my hand as we walk to the garage, a short stroll from the main house. The red brick structure makes up a square around a courtyard of workshops, stables, and other utility buildings. Jason unlocks the old wooden concertina door and pushes a portion back, which screeches with the effort of shifting. Inside, the air is still and musty. There's a lingering odor of oil, kerosine, leather, and beeswax polish. Various cans and pots are arranged on shelving around the walls and in the middle of the space a beige tarpaulin covers a large vehicle.

"Now. This, I might keep," says Jason with a grin as he pulls the cover from the glossy black and silver-gray panels of an enormous vintage car. "It's a 1953 Rolls-Royce Silver Dawn convertible."

"Oh my!" I gasp. "She's gorgeous."

"Yes, she is. And the motor still fires. It's amazing that all she needs is a tune-up. And her seats need a little upholstery work, but..."

I slowly walk around the classic car, which is double the length of Bertie, at least. Enormous headlights, the size of dinner plates, remind me of a frog. And at the front is an elegant sculpted shiny figurine of a woman with arms stretching out behind her in billowing fabric.

"She looks like a fairy," I say pointing at the little statuette.

"Ah, yes. The Spirit of Ecstasy. She's beautiful..." Jason pauses and looks into my eyes. "Like... the car."

I run my hands along the contours of the opulent vehicle, picturing me in the passenger seat beside Jason as we cruise along with the top down in dappled summer sunlight. I quickly shake the image away embarrassed by the clarity of my imagination.

"These machines were top of the range. Real statement pieces." Jason laughs. "I can imagine the guys at the exclusive golf club with their big old expensive cars parked out front. Maybe the chauffeurs polishing the headlights while they wait for their bosses to finish their game and maybe seal a business deal."

"Like *The Great Gatsby*." I complete the circuit of the Rolls-Royce and stand close to Jason. "You'll need a garage for her. Why not keep the garage as well as the car?"

"That would be fine, but I believe, from the real estate people, that everything here is going to be bulldozed for a new development."

"No!" The word comes out stronger and louder than necessary and ricochets around the garage space launching startled flapping pigeons from the roof. "Sorry. I mean, that's a shame."

"That's what happens, Charlie. You can't be sentimental about the past. Time moves on and new takes over from old. That's how the world is."

"It doesn't have to be that way, Jason." I'm disappointed as if I have a claim on what I see. This place isn't mine. Jason isn't anything more to me than a kind man in the right place at the right time. My imagination is running away with itself. I need to rein it in and get real. "I'm sure you'll get a good price for it."

The grand tour is over. I turn and push the doors open then walk out of the garage, gasping like a fish out of water. I'm sad and angry that the outcome for this grand old hotel is demolition. It doesn't seem right. Jason calls out somewhere behind me as I stride back to the main house, tears prickling my eyes. I find Maddie still playing princesses in the living room.

"I'm going now, Maddie," I say as the little girl reaches up to hug me.

"Why? You should stay and have tea with the Duke and Duchess. They've just arrived from Scotland and they're dying to meet you."

"Thanks, Maddie, but another time. I've got to go now."

Jason catches up with me in the hallway, but I can't look at him.

"Charlie, what's up?" he says, reaching for my arm but I pull away, shaking my head with sad disbelief.

I choke back a sob and almost run down the curved path to the gate where Bertie is parked. I jump in and drive away without looking back.

Chapter 17

Jason

"Fairy Charlie didn't stay to meet the Duke and Duchess from Scotland," Maddie says with sincere disappointment. "I laid out a place for her and everything."

She indicates the circle of little pretty tea things that surround her where she sits cross-legged on the floor. Maddie picks up one of the teacups with gold handles and pretends to drink from it. Then she eats a slice of pretend cake from a matching dainty plate decorated with roses. A teapot, empty milk jug, and sugar bowl are in the middle of the circle with a grand three-tiered cake stand.

"She had to go, Maddie," I explain. "But she'll come back and have tea with you… and the Duke and Duchess from Scotland, another time."

"Mmmm. Too late. They're only here to have tea with me today and then they have to go back to their castle."

"That's too bad."

"Yes. Fairy Charlie missed out on something very special."

Maddie's words ring around my head. *Missed out on something very special*. That is exactly the feeling I have just now. That I have missed out on something very special and rare and beautiful.

The jolt I felt as Charlie reached for my hand. The warmth of her fingers as they curled around mine. The incredible feeling that I never wanted to let her go as we walked together to the garage. And then something I said upset her and now she's gone. I clench my jaw and rub the back of my neck in disbelief. I'm experiencing a sense of loss for something I never had, which is ridiculous. I shake off my undue mushy emotions.

This big old house is getting to me. I've been here too long. I turn my attention back to Maddie who gallantly continues her pretend tea party despite her disappointment.

"Could you give me an ETD of the Duke and Duchess? We need to get moving soon. Okay?"

"They left already." Maddie shrugs and sighs. "I'm good to go now, Jason." She stands up and wipes pretend crumbs from her dress.

I scoop Maddie up and give her a hug and she wraps her arms around me. Then I put her down and she holds my hand as I switch off the lights and lock up the hotel. Then I turn on the security system I had installed, with cameras and an alarm that alerts a twenty-four-hour service. It's pricey but necessary for peace of mind. And it means that I'm not so tied to the place.

Rocko lopes on ahead as I walk with Maddie back to the gatehouse. He knows it's dinnertime.

"Hey, Rocko has a new collar," says Maddie with a bright smile which lifts my mood. "I like it. It can be his Sunday best collar; his Christmas collar; the collar he wears to go to a party."

I open the gatehouse door, but Maddie points to the bag and package stowed carefully on the shelf beside the tools.

"Charlie left them," I say by way of explanation.

"Aren't you going to open your present, Jason?"

I stop, hesitantly. "Yeah. Maybe later, huh? We've got to get going."

"How about now? It'll only take a couple of minutes. Unless it's a Christmas present and you want to bring it home and put it under our tree and open it with us on Christmas Day?"

I sigh, trying to ignore the Christmas comment. I don't tell Maddie that I'm planning to hide myself away again until the whole shebang is over. But Meredith still buys me a gift and will corner me when I turn up eventually, with what they call an un-Christmas. Just for me.

"No. I think it's a thank-you present, Maddie."

"Great, then you're totally allowed to open it right now."

I don't move. I stare at the package. Then I look at Maddie and say, "How about you open it for me?"

"How come you don't want to open your present? If it was my present I'd open it straight away. And I definitely wouldn't let anyone else open it for me."

"Okay, okay. I'll open it now." I take the package from the shelf. An envelope falls on the ground. I pick it up then push the door open and we all go inside. Maddie sits on the couch. Rocko jumps up beside her and I sit on the chair. I open the envelope and read the message which makes me smile.

"What does it say, Jason?"

"It says, Merry Christmas. I hope all your dreams come true. Then, Charlie says, if I ever want juggling lessons, to call her."

"Oh, how wonderful," squeals Maddie clapping her hands. "Open the present," she demands.

I peel off the ribbon and tear away the festive wrapping to reveal a box of three brightly colored soft balls. Rocko pricks up his ears and looks interested.

"No, Rocko. They're not for you."

"I think you should call Charlie and tell her how much you love your present and say yes to juggling lessons. What's in the bag?"

"Just the clothes Charlie borrowed when she stayed with me in the storm."

Memories of being snowed in together come flooding back and I don't know what to do with them. Images of Charlie in the candlelight; asleep on the couch; her sleepy face in the morning; the way she raced out and made snow angels; the way I stood there like an idiot.

"Get your things, Maddie. I'll feed Rocko, then we'll go."

I park in Meredith's driveway. Daniel, my brother-in-law, comes out to greet us.

"Daddy!" yells Maddie, loud and excited.

"Hey, Maddie, my darling," Daniel says opening the rear door of the Chevy. "I've missed you so much."

"I missed you, so much too," Maddie says as her dad unbuckles her from the back seat. "Jason got a present from fairy Charlie."

"That's nice. Who's fairy Charlie?"

"You know, Daddy. She was at Isabel's party, then she had a sleepover with Jason."

"It wasn't a sleepover, Maddie. There was a storm. She was stuck there with me."

I watch as a lightbulb pings on in Daniel's head. "Oh, that fairy Charlie. Please come in and tell me all about it."

I follow Daniel and Maddie into the house which is festooned with Christmas decorations. A huge tree takes up most of the space in the living room.

"That's new since I was last here." My comment about the tree is a deliberate deflection from the subject of fairies. "How was Washington, Daniel?"

"Ha! Frustrating mostly. A lot of talk and not much action. Thankfully, I got away earlier than expected. But enough about that. It's Christmas and I'm back here with my best girl." Daniel picks up Maddie, squeezes her close, and dances in a circle on the carpet which makes Maddie giggle. "You've grown so much, Maddie. How come my little girl has got so big so quick?"

Meredith appears in the doorway wiping her hands on a tea towel, quietly watching her husband and daughter laughing.

"Come on, I've made some gingerbread cookies," she says smiling warmly as we walk to the kitchen.

"Fairy Charlie, huh? What's going on there, do you think?"

Meredith scoops out some frosting and fills a piping bag. The countertop is almost completely covered with person-shaped gingerbread cookies which smell mouth-wateringly delicious. I put my hand out to take one, but Meredith slaps it away, then she fixes me with a stern look.

"She stopped by with a thank-you gift," I say as casually as I can, hoping my churn of emotions isn't showing. "Which was nice and completely unnecessary."

Meredith doesn't say anything but holds the frosting bag nozzle steady over the first gingerbread man in the row.

"Really. She's nice." I sound too defensive. "And that's all." I shove my hands into the pockets of my jeans and look out of the window. "The gift was a nice thought."

Meredith looks up briefly from piping a smiley face onto another cookie. "And," she says.

Maddie comes into the kitchen followed by Daniel. He picks her up and sits her on one of the bar stools, then sits on the stool beside her.

"They look good enough to eat," says Daniel with his arm protectively around Maddie.

"Soon," says Meredith.

"We washed our hands and everything. Didn't we, Maddie?"

"Well, great. Maddie, do you want to decorate a cookie?" Meredith hands the frosting bag to Maddie and then gives her a plate with three gingerbread men on it.

"Alright," says Maddie seriously. "This one is you, Daddy." She pipes a smiley face onto one of the gingerbread men. She gives him a tie and buttons in a line down the middle. She pauses and says, "Did Jason tell you about the present?"

"No, Maddie." Meredith grins at me. "Not yet."

"Jason. Tell us about the present." Maddie continues to decorate the cookies. "It's the best," she says as she draws a smiley face on the next cookie. "This one's you, Mommy."

I look at the floor. "Juggling balls. Charlie got me juggling balls and wrote in the card to call her if I needed lessons."

"Ah! That's brilliant," says Daniel. "That really is a very good present."

Then, Meredith says, "I love her already. When can we meet her properly?"

"Ask her to come for Christmas, Jason," says Maddie as she draws messy zigzags on the last cookie on her plate. "This one is me."

"Now, hold on, just a minute." I put my hands out as if that's going to stop the wave of enthusiasm. "Charlie probably has plans for Christmas. And who says I need juggling lessons?"

"Well, can you juggle?" asks Meredith.

"No. But that doesn't mean I need lessons." I walk to the door and back again. "I may not have time… I may not want to."

"You don't want to learn to juggle?" Maddie is incredulous. "Come on. We can practice right now." My niece slides down off the barstool.

"Just a minute," says Daniel. "You need to wash your hands again."

"Oh yeah. I forgot." Maddie goes over to the sink where Meredith turns on the tap for her, then gives her a tea towel for drying. Maddie holds up her hands to her mom for inspection. Meredith gives her a nod of approval.

Then my niece leads me to the living room. She picks up the remote and turns on the TV, then flicks through the channel menu and finds YouTube.

"You can find lessons teaching you just about anything. This is how I learned my frosting skills." Maddie's expression is stony serious. "Alright, Jason. Go get your juggling balls and I'll find someone in here to show you how." Maddie looks up at me with eyebrows raised. "You don't want to go and get lessons from Charlie if you haven't even tried it on your own, do you?"

"Maddie. I don't have my gift. I left it back at the mansion."

"I know. I thought you just forgot to bring it. So, I brought it." Maddie doesn't take her eyes off the screen as she scrolls through 'Juggling for Beginners', 'Juggling 101', 'Juggling Made Simple', and a whole heap of others on a list that is making my head spin. "The box is in the car."

I stand for a moment trying to figure out how exactly to respond to this pint-sized dictator. Meredith and Daniel watch from the kitchen. They smile and shrug as if they are powerless to intervene.

Chapter 18

Charlie

I'm in the Sparkle Entertainers van with Lou and Calvin. We have a booking downtown tonight. It's a big corporate Christmas bash and we are providing part of the entertainment. Calvin and Lou are doing their Cirque Du Soleil style acrobatic/ magic show/ dance type performance that's scheduled after the canapes and before the band. I'm the roadie and dressed as a fairy. My job will be to make sure the performance space is set up with the props, so Lou and Calvin have what they need when they need it.

As we drive to the venue at a hotel event hall, we talk through the routine. It's not new but Calvin always likes to add something extra to make each performance unique and fresh.

"So, when Lou comes down from the ladder, that's when we'll do the cross-over juggling routine with the clubs, and then end off with the devil sticks with Lou on my shoulders. How does that sound?" Calvin slows down and changes gear to stop at a pedestrian crossing.

"Yep. Sounds good," says Lou who is in the middle of the seat between me and Calvin.

I mentally place the clubs and devil sticks at the side of an imaginary performance space. We won't know the exact dimensions or limitations until we get there, and we may need to alter the sequence accordingly. Lou and Calvin have been performing together for a few years and have developed a trust and bond that's strong and deep. I never tire of watching them on stage and seeing the audience react. It's amazing what they do.

As we pick up speed again, I gaze vacantly out of the window at the festive street filled with Christmas shoppers. I'm thinking about Jason and feeling sad.

As if Lou can read my mind, she says, "It's done, Charlie. You went. You saw Jason." She reaches over and gently squeezes my hand. "At least you know now. That's why you went, isn't it? To find out. One way or another. If there was a spark or if you just made the whole thing up."

"Yeah. At least now I know." I turn to my friend and force a smile.

The whole city is lit up and decorated like a Christmas tree. Seeing people hurry up and down carrying bags and boxes, buying the perfect gift for their loved ones lifts my heavy heart. It seems as if everyone is happy and full of Christmas spirit.

"Sorry. I don't know why it got to me, but it did," I say brightly. "And... Jason and I... Yes. The spark is there. I know he's feeling it too. It's insane how close I feel." I pause as I remember his hand gently holding mine. "Felt. Past tense." Somewhere on the street outside a mechanical version of Jingle Bells plays a tinny serenade as we pass. "It all stopped when we were talking in the garage about the big old car, and I had this..." I laugh to admit my romantic idiocy. "I imagined us driving along with the top down, and I just felt so happy. Now, I feel stupid because I've projected all my silliness and big ideals on that poor man. He doesn't deserve it and..." I grab Lou's hand and squeeze it back. "He's nice... He definitely has issues, for sure. No doubt about that. But he's not for me." I shake my head. "I see that now."

"You sound pretty sure, Charlie," says Calvin checking the illuminated green line on the sat nav.

"I think I just realized when we were talking about what was going to happen to the hotel, I felt so sad and disappointed. It's just a classic, *It's not him. It's me.* scenario." I laugh. "We are just so different."

"Different is good," says Calvin. "You know, yin and yang. You can be different and complement each other."

"'You complete me'," Lou leans across and kisses Calvin's cheek. "Like in Jerry Maguire, Charlie."

"Yeah, but we couldn't be more opposite. And we're not simply opposites. We are on completely different planets." I sigh. "How did I ever think we could connect at all?" I pause for a moment. "And I know I sound absurd, but I don't know if I want to be with someone who is obviously so soulless they want to give up that house." I shake my head again and laugh some more. "And let's not forget, he didn't even want to make a snow angel."

The van is quiet for a moment, then Calvin says, "He's practical, Charlie." He slows down and indicates to make a turn. "And that's a good thing, isn't it? You can understand why he wants to sell. It must be a huge responsibility. And really expensive."

"I know. And the land value is worth more without the building. How crazy is that? But it's such a beautiful place.

You should see it before it's torn down. Then you'll know what I mean."

"You don't think that maybe he'll change his mind and... I don't know, keep the hotel?" says Lou hopefully.

"No. I can't see that ever happening. He's already said he's not that person and he never will be. You guys haven't met him yet. And you probably never will now."

Then Lou says, "But Charlie, you invited him for Christmas dinner, didn't you?"

"Yes. But he won't come. I mean think about it. Why would he?"

"We'll see," says Lou. "Stranger things have happened. Don't forget, it's Christmas and that's when all sorts of magic happens."

"Lou. Christmas magic happens in the show. And nowhere else. Oh, apart from in the movies."

Lou laughs at me as Calvin indicates a turn into the hotel parking lot. He checks the rearview and pulls the van to a stop. I open the van door and slide out followed by Lou. Time to get into performance mode and stop thinking about something that is absolutely out of reach. I grab the gear from the back of the van and we wait for our contact from the booking. Soon a smartly suited young man with an iPad approaches us. He looks us up and down.

"Hello. I'm Tim. And you must be Sparkle Entertainers. I'll show you to the dressing room." He checks the time. "You'll find the run sheet I emailed you in there. Let me know if you need anything." His hand darts up to an earpiece but he keeps walking briskly. He nods a couple of times then he says, "The dressing rooms are just through here. The green room is at the end. Help yourself to refreshments." He pauses to listen to his earpiece again, then says, "Excuse me, one moment." He pushes open a door with a restricted access sign. "I'll be right back."

Lou, Calvin, and I watch him scurry away to where a crew of people dressed in black arrange balloons and decorations and rig lighting equipment onto scaffolding bars. Someone is testing the sound, *one, two, one, two*.

"It would be so awesome to…" I begin voicing a thought.

"To what, Charlie," asks Lou who is close enough to hear.

"Ah, nothing. Just an idea." I smile at my friends and shake the thought away. It's time to concentrate on the evening's show.

Chapter 19

Jason

When I call Charlie's number it clicks straight through to voicemail. I hesitate. I really want to talk to her and not a stupid machine. But then, I end up leaving a message, as instructed, after the beep.

"Hi, it's Jason. I just wanted to say thanks for the juggling balls. Maddie's been helping me. Anyway, I would love it if you called me back. I know you must be busy fairying somewhere. So..." I hang up. I want to erase the message immediately. *Busy fairying?* No one says that.

It's no surprise that I don't get a call back. I've stopped checking my phone every five minutes. But I've been thinking, and I've had a crazy idea. And I need to talk to Charlie about it. I think she can help. But mostly, I just want to talk to her. I miss her so much. I'm going to ask her out on a date. Take her for a ride in the Rolls-Royce or something fun. I don't know. Do something to make her smile. I couldn't bear the look she gave me when she left the mansion. She was so upset. It broke my heart to think it was me and something that I said that made her so miserable. I want us to be friends. I want us to be more than friends.

I call Meredith. I'm not sure how she's going to react to my idea. I'm a little apprehensive as I dial my sister's number, but she'll give me a straight answer and let me know, honestly, if she thinks I'm mad. Meredith picks up straight away.

"Hey, Sis. What are you up to?" I say over-brightly.

"Well, Jason. I'm baking some more gingerbread cookies."

"More cookies, huh?"

"Yes. Of course. They make great gifts. Who wouldn't want a stack of Christmas gingerbread men all decorated with frosting and shiny colored sugar beads?" There's a pause on the line. "Maddie says you should come and decorate them with us."

"Thanks, but I'm busy with something here at the mansion." I lean back on the couch and watch the flames in the wood stove. "But have fun with that."

Maybe this isn't the right time and I'm about to hang up when Meredith says, "Okay, Jason. So why the call?"

"Ah yes. I wanted to run an idea by you. It concerns the sale of the mansion, so I need your take on it."

"Okay. What's in your head?"

I take a deep breath. "You know the plan for the mansion was always to sell up as fast as possible?"

"Yes."

"Well. I've had an idea. It might sound crazy, and I know we agreed that it's a money pit and we should just get rid."

"I'm listening."

"But what if we didn't sell? What if we did something cool with it?"

Meredith laughs. "Like what?"

I'm out of my comfort zone but I push through and say, "Like a hotel. But more of a venue. For weddings and stuff."

"Stop right there. Who are you and what have you done with my brother?" Meredith laughs some more. "Jason, since when were you interested in doing up an old house? And since when were you ever interested in weddings?"

"Since I learned to juggle."

"Excuse me?"

"Look it's hard to explain. I've just had a blinding, what-do-you-call-it? When your life and everything you thought was real just isn't?"

"An epiphany."

"Alright. Yes. That's it."

"Are you going to shave your head and start wearing orange? You'd look good by the way."

"No. Nothing like that. But I do feel as if I've seen the light. Sort of."

"Good gracious. Jason. Are you in love?"

"I don't know. I need to figure things out. But, maybe..."

"It's the fairy, isn't it? The one you got stuck with in the blizzard. Charlie." There's a pause as I think about what to say. "Ha. Your silence says it all. When can we meet her?"

"I don't know," I say stroking Rocko's ears and thinking about Charlie. I don't know what to tell my sister.

"Are you still there? Jason?"

"Yes." I sigh. "Meredith. I don't want to sell the mansion. But I know you were counting on the money, so we need to talk about what that means for all of us."

"Okay. Jason. Let's start with you, then. What would it mean for you, if you didn't sell? Could you put your career on hold? Would it mean that you're going to stop being an engineer and stay in one place? Can you do that? Do you think?"

"I can try." Rocko jumps down and lies on the floor in front of the stove. "We have an opportunity to do something cool with this place that could generate cash. There is so much to tell you, but…"

"Yes. I want to hear all about it. Wow, this is a complete turnaround, Jason. But I trust you. I'm overwhelmed. Gosh. What happens now?"

"Well. I'll contact the real estate agent and stop that process from going any further. Meredith. I'd like to see if what I imagine is possible. And if it is, and we can make a successful business, then wouldn't that be exciting?"

"So exciting!"

"We'll give it a go and if it doesn't work out, we can still sell up, but only after we've given our best shot." The phone line is quiet.

Strangely, voicing my idea to Meredith makes my mad dream seem plausible. I have this notion of something I know absolutely nothing about. I'm excited. I'm terrified.

"So why the change of heart? Is this Charlie's idea?"

"No. She doesn't know yet. I called but she hasn't called me back." I sigh but then I go on hoping to redirect Meredith away from Charlie. "Listen. I've been finding out about the hotel and the people who lived here, and I just don't feel as if I can let it be bulldozed. It doesn't seem right to destroy a legacy. I feel a responsibility to keep their story alive. Out of respect, but also…"

"So, you're telling me that this has nothing to do with Charlie?"

"Okay. I'd be lying if I said no. But she may not want anything to do with me. She hasn't called back. I left a message. Meredith. I think I've blown it there. I don't know."

"But she invited you for Christmas dinner, didn't she?"

"Yes."

"So go."

"I don't know. People say and do things they don't mean. Charlie felt sorry for me living in this big old place alone." Rocko rolls onto his back and begins to snore. "She's kind and I'm a charity case."

"Maybe. Maybe not. Go find out. But come to us first, okay? I'm sure Daniel will want to hear about your plans. And bring Rocko, okay?" Meredith hangs up the call.

Chapter 20

Charlie

"Merry Christmas!" Calvin pulls a cracker with Lou as George Michael sings his classic on the sound system Christmas playlist. We laugh as the shiny cardboard rips. A slip of paper falls out with an orange plastic whistle and a pink party hat. Lou picks up the party hat, unfolds it, and puts it on. Calvin picks up the whistle and blows it, then unwraps the mini pack of playing cards from the previous cracker, clearly delighted with the dinky prizes.

"Ah, a joke," Lou says clearing her throat in preparation for theatrical effect. "What do elves do after school?"

"We don't know," Calvin and I chime in together. "What do elves do after school?"

"Their gnome work!"

We all groan collectively. "Honestly. These get worse every year," says Calvin.

"Where did you get these?" asks Lou.

"Ah, they're left over from that corporate event downtown last week," I say, sipping from my glass of mimosa. "Remember Tim, the organizer? He handed me a goody bag on the way out and the crackers were part of the swag."

"Excellent. Cool. Cheers," says Lou. "Got to love a big-budget gig."

"It's my go," I say, carefully putting my glass down.

"Oh, well, we don't have any more of those crackers left, but this box was sent to the office." Calvin hands me a cardboard box with pictures of crackers on the top and the sides. "It's actually addressed to you, Charlie. Looks deluxe. Special."

"Ah, yeah. It's probably from the family, that we did the wizard party for, who were let down at the last minute. Do you remember? They were so grateful when I said we could step in."

"Yeah. Vaguely," says Lou before she sips her mimosa.

"There must be a mistake," I say, laughing, as I open the box. Strangely, there's only one cracker inside. "Where are the others?"

I take out the lone cracker, hold one end, and offer the other end to Lou. We tug at the same time causing a crack and more ripped paper. As expected, another party hat falls out. This time it's lime green. I unfold it and put it on. Then I shake my end of the cardboard tube, and a little box, tied with ribbon, drops on the table with a thin slip of paper.

"How intriguing," says Calvin leaning over to get a better look.

I pick up the box, then uncurl the piece of paper, and read what's written on it.

"Tell us another appalling joke, Charlie," says Lou giggling.

"It's not a joke. It's a Christmas wish."

"What?"

"That's what it says here. It's a rhyme." I begin to read out loud.

If what you wish for is the same as me.
This gift cannot be found under the Christmas tree.
Look inside your heart.
That is where your wish might be.

"How odd," says Lou taking the flimsy piece of paper from my hand. "What does it mean?"

Lou looks at Calvin who shrugs and says, "That family must have you confused with someone else, I think."

I stare into space as an idea slaps me. "I think it's from Jason," I say quietly as I reach for my mimosa and take a swift slurp.

"Really?"

"Open the box," Lou demands.

I pull the ribbon from the square cardboard package and carefully take the lid off. Inside is something sparkly wrapped in pink tissue. I take it out and peel away the layer of thin paper.

"It's a bracelet," I say turning the dainty string of glittery stones arranged in a series of flowers over in my hand.

"So pretty," says Lou with twinkly eyes. Then she says, "Well, if it is from Jason. How do you feel about that?"

"I don't know. I'm surprised. I love it." I put the bracelet on and admire how it sparkles. "It's just so unexpected. I mean, we haven't really connected since that day at the mansion. He left a message, but I haven't called him back."

"It could mean that he's had a change of heart," says Calvin topping up our glasses with what's left of bubbly wine.

"Call him."

"No. It might not be from Jason. Anyway, he'll be with his sister and..."

"Well. He might just turn up. You did invite him for Christmas dinner, remember?"

"Speaking of which," Calvin says as he stands up holding his glass. "I should get busy in the kitchen." He leaves Lou and me in the living room, sipping his mimosa as he goes.

We clear the debris of Christmas wrapping from the floor. Then Lou goes to the kitchen to help Calvin as I lay the table and arrange the candle centerpiece.

I pause to look at the pretty bracelet again and hold it up to the light. A warm glow fills me as I think about Jason, the most practical, sensible person I have ever met. And the consideration and effort that went into my gift. Maybe I read him all wrong. I had him pegged as a dry, decidedly unromantic man who would never understand me. The bracelet proves that there's much more going on than I first thought. If the gift is from Jason, that is.

I light the candles on the dining table and admire the cozy living room with all its tinsel and twinkly lights. Nat King Cole sings about roasting chestnuts on an open fire and I feel all tingly inside - the sort of tingles that only happen at Christmastime. Then I realize that Nat King Cole is my phone ringing and not the track on the Christmas playlist. The device vibrates and lights up on the bookshelf, where I left it, beside the mini-Santa in his sleigh pulled by some very life-like reindeer.

I pick up my phone and answer without checking caller ID.

"Hey, Charlie. It's Jason."

I gasp in surprise. My heart is about to burst, but manage to say, "Ah, Jason. Merry Christmas. How are you?" I'm nervous and gabbling. "Are you having a nice time? Is Rocko wearing his Christmas collar? Where are you spending your day? At the mansion? Is it cold up there?"

"No." Jason laughs. "I was at Meredith's this morning, but now I'm right outside your place."

Still holding my phone I hurry to the window and peek out through the drapes. Jason is standing on the path. Snowflakes fall softly. He's holding a big bag decorated with Christmas angels. I'm stunned for a minute by the magical scene, then drop my phone on the couch and rush to open the door. Christmas tingles are now heart-fluttering jitters. I fling open the door but almost slam it shut again.

Then I get it together enough to say, "Hello, Jason. What a surprise."

"Is it?" Jason smiles at me through the falling snow. "You invited me. I have the card here, just in case you forgot." Jason holds up the Christmas card that I had given him with the juggling balls. "It is Christmas day. And I guess it is coming up to dinner time. So, here I am."

I shiver in the evening chill. "Jason. I can't believe you're here." My breath appears in clouds. "Come in. Please." I step aside to allow Jason to pass, then close the door.

"You didn't return my call, so I really only had one option, Charlie," Jason says shyly as he follows me into the living room where the table is set for four. "It is still okay for me to…"

"Yes. Yes, of course. I'm just, um." I shrug. "I didn't think you'd come. That's all."

"If you'd rather I left," Jason says moving back toward to front door.

"No. No. Please. Let me take your coat. Have a seat and… Can I get you a drink? Egg nogg? Coke? Tea?" I try and think of other drinks and beverages I can offer. "We're having mimosas. I could get you one of those."

"Yeah. A mimosa would be great. But make it orange juice heavy. I'm driving."

"Sure." I'm breathless. "One sec." I run to the kitchen. "Guess what?" I hiss at my roommates.

"What?"

"It's Jason. He's here." I point wildly behind me. "In the living room. He wants a mimosa." I slump against the doorframe. "He's come for dinner. And it's snowing!"

"That's great, Charlie. Go," says Lou ushering me from the kitchen. "I'll bring the drinks."

I take a deep breath before casually walking back to the living room. I sit beside Jason on the couch. The Christmas angel bag is on the floor beside him. There's an awkward pause before I turn to him and ask, "Did you send one Christmas cracker in a box addressed to me?"

"I see you got it." Jason takes my hand and looks at the bracelet. "It looks really nice. I was hoping that you'd like it. Maddie helped me choose. It belonged to Great Aunt Alice. She's wearing it in the photo at my place. Do you remember?"

"Ah. Yes. I love it. Thank you so much." I slowly turn my wrist to admire the sparkling stones. "It's so special." Then, I say, "And the cracker. What did you mean? The poem?"

Jason opens his mouth to reply but he is interrupted by Lou and Calvin who come in holding trays of drinks and plates of canapés.

"Hey. Merry Christmas," Lou says placing her tray on the table. Jason stands up to greet her. "You must be Jason," she says. "I'm Lou and this is Calvin. I'm so pleased that you made it. Perfect timing, by the way." She smiles. "Dinner's almost ready."

"Thanks for having me." Jason shakes hands with Calvin.

Lou hands round the glasses, and we stand together by the tree and say, "Cheers! Merry Christmas." Our glasses clink together, then we all take a sip, before sitting at the table. Lou is beside Calvin, and I sit opposite, next to Jason.

"Maddie must have been so pleased you were there today," I say thinking about the little girl opening her presents.

"Yes. She says, hi, and Merry Christmas. And she wants me to bring you to meet Meredith and Daniel soon. It's the rules, apparently." There's a pause in the conversation as we sip our drinks. "That reminds me," Jason says standing up and walking toward the big Christmassy bag. "These are from Meredith." He pulls out a small cellophane mountain tied up with a shiny red bow. "She hopes you like gingerbread." Jason brings the gift to the table.

"I love gingerbread," say Lou and Calvin together.

Then Calvin says, "So, the mansion." He leans forward on his elbows, his fingers interlaced in front of him on the table. "Charlie says it's a wonderful old building. Used to be a hotel."

"That's right. It's definitely grand." Jason leans back and rests his arm across the back of my chair. "And it has a history of colorful characters who have stayed there."

"And you're planning to sell it?" says Lou inquisitively.

"I was. But..." Jason breathes deeply then leans forward and turns to face me. "I wanted to run something by you, Charlie." His eyes meet mine. They are soft and bright in the candlelight. Then Jason looks across from Lou to Calvin and says, "Well, all of you, actually."

No one interrupts and we wait for Jason to continue. Michael Jackson sings 'Santa Claus is Coming to Town', the next tune on the Christmas playlist.

"I don't have a clue about this kind of thing, so I was wondering what you think about maybe turning the place into a venue." Jason smiles. "I know it sounds crazy. But I don't want to sell up now." Jason bites his lip before he goes on. "If I can generate enough cash somehow, I don't know, but I want to keep it."

"Really?" I blurt out. "You want to stay there?"

"Yes, I really do. I told my agent to hold off job offers for now. And I've taken the property off the market until I can figure out what I'm doing."

"Wow! That's so exciting," says Lou, her eyes shining.

"Exciting is one way to describe it," Jason says. "But I'm actually terrified. I have no idea what I'm doing." He laughs and I reach for his hand and cover it with mine. "It's scary but I feel as if I'm doing the right thing." He turns toward me, but I don't see fear in his eyes or someone with an unwanted burden. This is not the gruff, impersonal man who begrudgingly rescued me from the side of the road. "I only know about engines and how they work. But hospitality and entertainment? And marketing and publicity? These things are alien to me. I wouldn't know where to start." He looks into my eyes and smiles. "I was hoping you could help me."

"Yes! Yes, of course. How brilliant," says Calvin. "I can't wait to have a look around."

"I'm sure there's a whole lot of potential for all sorts," says Lou.

"Rocko!" I exclaim. "Where is he?"

Jason laughs and holds my hand up to his lips. He kisses it gently.

"I left him with Meredith. Don't worry."

"I thought he was all alone at the mansion. I couldn't bear that." I cover my mouth with my other hand. "Okay. Sorry. What were you saying?"

Everyone laughs. Then Calvin and Lou bring in plates piled high with a vegetarian Christmas feast. A nut roast with all the trimmings and onion gravy. We eat and chat about other things. It feels wonderful to have Jason with me. I steal a sideways look his way.

He holds my gaze for a moment, then he says, "This really is wonderful food," as he maneuvers another forkful of sweet potato toward his mouth. "I've never had a vege Christmas before."

"Something tells me that you'd better get used to it," Lou says with a cheeky wink.

Chapter 21

Jason

I was so surprised that I enjoyed a vegetarian Christmas dinner. And I feel so at home and welcome at Charlie's place. Lou and Calvin are the friendliest people.

After dinner, Charlie and I take the plates to the kitchen, wash the dishes, and tidy up. We chat away as if we do this all the time. I mention this fact to Charlie, who blushes as she takes a plate from the dish rack, dries it with a tea towel, and puts it away on the shelf.

"We hardly know each other," she says still blushing. She sweeps her fringe away from her eyes with the back of her hand.

"This is true," I say washing another plate. "But like what you said at my place in the storm, I like what I know so far." I smile at Charlie. "And I'd like to get to know you more. So, here's the thing, unless you supply me with detailed documentation, I think the best way of getting to know someone is to share time with them. Or am I being hopelessly optimistic and old-fashioned?"

Charlie laughs and says, "No. I think sharing time with you would be fine. And..." She stops and bites her lip, then smiles back at me. "Jason."

"Yep." I scrub a handful of silverware and put it on the dish rack to drain, then pause to wait for Charlie to continue.

"I am so happy that you're not selling the mansion." She wipes the counter. "I was upset by the thought of that beautiful grand old place being torn down." Charlie stops wiping the counter and turns to face me, holding the tea towel at her chest as if she's praying. "I just felt the loss of something irreplaceable right here in my heart." She frowns at me with sad eyes. "That's why I didn't call you back. I was just so sad." She turns to wipe the counter again. "It's none of my business, of course. I mean, what you do with your inheritance is..."

"No. I understand. I felt that too." I splosh clean water on another plate and place it on the dish rack. "I spent so long thinking about the sensible choices, the figures on the page, and what the money would mean to Meredith and Maddie. I didn't see what was right in front of me." I lift my soapy hands from the water in a useless comic gesture and shake my head. "Charlie. When you came to see me and we got the gramophone going and I showed you around the house, it dawned on me what a treasure it is." I wash another plate. "And finding out about Great Aunt Alice and her story. She was quite a character by all accounts." Charlie listens intently as I say all the things I've been wanting to tell her. "But I'm a practical man. And being me, I didn't want to give in to my emotions." I laugh as I think about what the mansion means to me now. "To hang on to the house makes no economic sense. It's a massive financial gamble. And to not sell it would also mean a huge lifestyle change for me." I pause to frame my thoughts. "Charlie. Remember when we were at the mansion, and you asked me about my best life. 'What is that?' you said." I reach for the roasting tin and begin to scrub it with the brush. "I couldn't answer because I didn't know how. I thought I knew what my best life looked like. But that was before I moved into the mansion. And it was before I met you." My eyes meet Charlie's which are soft and searching. She doesn't interrupt, so I go on. "I didn't know how to respond. I didn't know anymore because so much had changed. The life I had been living - from contract to contract, from place to place - just didn't seem fulfilling anymore. It was a life I didn't want to go back to. And, until you asked me, I hadn't considered how irrelevant it was." I smile at Charlie because I'm aware that I've been talking for a while, but I need her to hear me. "So, I had this internal battle going on between Jason, practical, sensible, makes decisions based on facts and figures, and this new Jason who... Gosh. I hardly know who he is, but this new Jason has taken over and is ready to take a massive risk with a falling-down hotel. And, Charlie. That's all because of you." I laugh. "Yes. I am blaming you. It's all your fault."

Charlie's eyes crinkle at the edges and she puts her hand to her mouth to hide her shy smile. "Hearing you say this changes everything. Jason. You have no idea how much this changes everything."

Charlie starts to giggle. She drops the tea towel on the counter. Her eyes are wide and shining with wonder. I desperately want to kiss her, but my hands are wet and soapy and still in the sink.

"I'm sorry," I say with urgency. "I need to do something now that's very important and I don't want it to be here in the kitchen when we're doing the dishes." I grab the tea towel and dry my hands. "Come on." I reach for Charlie and lead her out of the kitchen and through to the living room where Lou and Calvin are playing a game with a tiny pack of cards. I walk to the bag that I brought with me and find the juggling balls.

"I suggest you stand back," I say with serious determination. "I'm just a beginner."

Lou and Calvin pause their game and look up with mild interest. Charlie stands in the doorway. I assess that I'll have adequate space to do what I've been practicing.

I take a deep inhalation and blow it out to focus my concentration, then I toss one of the balls into the air in front of me. The first ball is followed by another tossed with the other hand. As the first ball descends, I toss the third and catch the first one with the same hand. This simple rotating action seems easy enough in theory, but the hand-eye coordination, and remembering to not hold my breath, have taken a lot of practice. My basic display is, inevitably short-lived, as all the balls, one by one, drop to the floor.

"Bravo!" calls Calvin who stands up to applaud enthusiastically. Lou whistles loudly and Charlie has covered her mouth with her hands but her shoulders quake with laughter. She finally shakes her head and comes over to hug me.

"Please. Charlie. I'd like to schedule some lessons," I say ignoring the colorful juggling balls, lying where they fell, at my feet. "If you have the time and patience for me."

"I don't know what to say," she says as I take her in my arms. It feels so good to hold her. I bury my face in her hair and breathe in her scent of cinnamon, pine needles, and strawberries.

"Do you want a job?" says Lou hugging Calvin. "We're always on the lookout for new talent."

"I know what the Christmas poem means now," Charlie says, breaking away from me and looking into my eyes. "You don't need to explain." I hold her hands. "This is the best Christmas ever."

"Do you know what would make it even better?" I say reaching for my jacket that is lying over the arm of the couch.

"Nothing could make it better, Jason." Charlie is grinning from ear to ear. She sparkles with happiness.

"No?" I smile, holding up a sprig of mistletoe that's a little bit squashed from being in the jacket pocket. "I wasn't sure if you had any, so I brought some, just in case." I hold up the misshapen stick of smooshed leaves and white berries, a little embarrassed about the state of it. But I'm in the moment and feel that this is my destiny. There's no turning back. "Charlie. You're so beautiful... You have changed my life in the most magical way, and I would very much like to kiss you now." I pause to take a breath. "If that's alright."

"Yes please," Charlie says quietly turning her face up to mine. I bend down to gently place my lips on hers which are soft and warm and feel exactly as I hoped they would.

But an unexpected jolt, like an electric shock, shoots from my lips to my toes and fingertips and back again causing me to break away and say, "Whoa!"

Somewhere in the background, Lou and Calvin whistle and cheer.

Chapter 22

Charlie

It's New Year's Eve. Lou, Calvin, and I have just arrived at the Mansion Hotel. It's the first time since Christmas Day that I've seen Jason. We've called each other, but we've both been too busy to meet up. I'm aching to see him and so excited. Not only about seeing Jason again but to be here with Lou and Calvin and to discuss plans for the future of this grand old historic house.

Rocko bounds to the gate when the van pulls up outside, closely followed by Jason who waves and smiles as he strides down the sweep of the driveway.

"Welcome!" he says unhooking the chain and opening the gates for us. Calvin drives through and parks next to Jason's Chevy.

Even before Calvin has cut the engine, I jump out and run back to throw my arms around my hunky hero. Jason bends to wrap me in a bear hug. Then he scoops me off my feet and we kiss madly, deeply, with wild passion until Lou and Calvin remind us that we have company. They shout and wave from the van as Rocko circles looking for a way in.

"Don't be scared," says Jason still holding me tightly with both arms. "Rocko's a big softy."

Calvin and Lou gingerly climb out of the van to make friends with Jason's massive dog. Rocko leans against their legs and nuzzles his face in their hands.

"Some guard dog, huh?" says Lou looking relieved.

"Come on," says Jason. "I'll show you the monstrous money pit."

"Or the potential goldmine?" I add laughing as our feet crunch on the gravel path toward the main entrance.

"It's certainly impressive from the outside," says Calvin looking up at the rows of elegant windows above.

"Wait until you get inside," I say smiling. "But I'm not going to say any more about it. I'll just let the house speak for itself."

Jason turns the handle and pushes open the front door. We gather in the hallway under the multi-tiered chandelier, which still sparkles beneath a layer of dust. Lou and Calvin instinctively gaze up to admire it suspended from the decorative ceiling high over our heads.

"This is definitely the statement welcome," Calvin says admiring the dimensions of the hall. "Full of wow factor, alright. An amazing space. I can already imagine the photos on the website. We'll have bookings coming out of our ears in no time."

"I love the old-fashioned reception desk," says Lou walking closer to admire the polished carved mahogany. "Look at the keys hanging up and the cubby holes for each room. It's this kind of authentic detail you can't recreate."

"The main living room is right here," says Jason, still holding my hand, as he leads us through the double door to the living room and the wall of windows and glass doors that open onto the terrace.

"It's huge," says Lou. "And I love the high ceiling. Gosh. I wouldn't change anything about this space. It's the perfect party room. What do you think, Cal?"

"Absolutely. I'm blown away. My head is so full of ideas about what we can do here." Calvin walks to the window and looks out at the gardens. "I mean. Jason. Before we even begin to market this as a venue, there's a whole heap of red tape and certifications we'll need to address." He paces as he says, "We'll need to create a timeframe and list all the things that need to be signed off before we can accept bookings." Calvin walks around checking items off on his fingers. "Fire department. Liquor license. Registration for the number of guests we can accommodate. The kitchen needs to be certified too, if food is prepared on the premises. But honestly, it's all doable, as long as the basic structure of the building is solid. So, a structural report is probably the first thing on the list."

We're quiet for a moment, as each of us is lost in our own thoughts. The wild ideas and practical realities settle into a cohesive form. There's no doubt about the effort and work in bringing the utilities up to an acceptable standard. But the important element we all agree on is keeping the feel of the grand old house: the history and stories of the people who lived here are as important as the bricks and mortar.

Jason opens one of the glass doors out onto the paved terrace. Wizened brown sticks are all that are left of plants in Grecian-type urns placed at pleasing intervals along the edge. Steps lead down to an overgrown lawn and rectangular pond reflecting an ornamental archway that promises to be covered in climbing roses during the summer months.

"There's a fountain in the middle but I'm not sure it works," says Jason almost apologetically. "I haven't tried it."

"That would be very cool," says Lou with infectious exuberance. "Imagine a fountain as a backdrop to your wedding photos. People would line up for that, wouldn't they?" She grins at me, then Jason. Then she looks at Calvin, who is suddenly serious. "Cal? Are you okay?"

Calvin doesn't answer straight off. He walks a few paces to the end of the terrace, then turns and walks back patting down the sides of his jacket. Then he gently takes Lou's hand, and breathing deeply, kneels down in front of her.

"Louise Bethany. You are the best thing in my life." Calvin reaches his free hand into his pocket. "I've been waiting for the right moment to ask." He pulls out a ring. "And I'm pretty sure that this is it." He smiles up at Lou who looks as if she might cry. "Lou. You are my world. Please. Please marry me."

Lou is stunned. Tears well up in her eyes, but she smiles and holds out her left hand, fingers outstretched.

"Yes. Calvin Adam. Yes. I'll marry you. I would be honored to be your wife."

Calvin looks up at Lou's smiling face and places the ring on her finger, then stands and takes both her hands in his. Jason hugs me and we turn away as they kiss.

"Enough, enough," I say rushing over to break up my smooching friends with hugs and kisses of my own. We stand together laughing for a few minutes before anyone speaks. Then it's Calvin who breaks away.

"Imagine if she had said no?" He laughs, taking Lou's hand again and pressing it to his lips. "Listen. It's just a thought. And, I don't know what you think about this, Lou, but Jason, how would you feel about us getting married here? What do you think?"

"Ah. Perfect. Just perfect," Lou jumps up to squeeze her fiancé, then she turns to Jason. "Could we?"

"It would be the most beautiful wedding," I say barely containing my happiness. "And to have it right here. Wouldn't that be perfect?"

"Wow. I'm speechless," says Jason, eventually. "I would love it. And you'd be the first wedding in the newly re-opened Mansion Hotel."

Rocko who has been lounging nearby, senses our excitement and ambles over, wagging his tail.

"I think we should try out the Rolls-Royce," Jason says putting an arm around my shoulders. "Who wants to go for a ride?"

Lou claps her hands as we make our way to the garage. "The Rolls-Royce will be perfect for weddings. I mean, who wouldn't want a ride in a vintage Rolls convertible?"

"At least there's one thing I feel confident about, that I can do," Jason says unlocking the garage door. "Tinkering with engines is my thing. The wedding and event stuff. That's up to you."

The rest of the afternoon is spent riding in the big old car, exploring the house and gardens, and talking about the amazing experiences we could offer our guests. There is so much to do before we even consider advertising, but the stage is set. Jason, Lou, Calvin, and I are abuzz with ideas and dreams. Getting the hotel ready to receive guests will take a few months, at least. But, with the tasks shared out, everyone can see a bright future for a dilapidated unloved house that was so close to demolition.

"Hey," says Lou as we walk back to the van in the chilly semi-darkness of early evening. "We're going to a New Year's party at a warehouse downtown later."

"Are you performing tonight?" asks Jason with his arms around me.

"No. We made a rule not to work at New Year's," says Calvin laughing and reaching for Lou. "It's some friends of ours, at their place. There'll be a DJ and a band, and it'll be fun. You should come too."

Jason seems suddenly shy. "I'll pass," he says standing beside me holding my hand. "I think I want to welcome the New Year right here. With Rocko." Then he looks across at me. "And you, Charlie. If you'd like to stay?" I'm so surprised, I don't say anything. I just stare back, wide-eyed. Then, Jason goes on hurriedly to fill in the silence. "Of course, I understand. It's New Year. And it's a party downtown with your friends. It'll be fun. For sure."

"No," I say gazing up at Jason's handsome face. His eyes meet mine in the soft twilight. "I'd love to stay here with you." Then I throw my arms around Jason's neck and squeal with delight. "It might snow. We might lose power. We might be stuck here! Yay!"

Lou and Calvin laugh. Jason picks me up and swings me around as if I'm a ragdoll.

When he puts me back down on my feet he says, "Well, there's enough food and I have a bottle of Moet chilling in the fridge."

"And let's get the gramophone and a stack of 78s," I say laughing.

"Well, that's settled," says Calvin climbing into the driver's seat of the van. "Sounds like you guys are going to have the best party, right here."

"Happy New Year," says Lou hugging me and then Jason before getting into the passenger seat.

"Happy New Year!" I shout and wave as the van's taillights disappear down the road and around the corner.

It's quiet and I'm alone with Jason in the dark. But I'm not stuck this time. We walk hand in hand to the tiny gatehouse.

"Where's the mistletoe?" I ask on the porch as Jason reaches for the door handle. I bite my lip and put my hands deep into my jacket pockets.

Jason pauses and faces me in the half-light. "Do we need mistletoe?" He steps toward me; his breath warms my cheek.

"I guess not," I say sliding under Jason's arm and standing with my back against the door.

Jason leans against me with one hand above my head, the other snaking around my waist under my jacket. We sense rather than see each other. I feel his gentle surrender as his lips meet mine. Our bodies meld together, entwining in a spiral of kissing pleasure. I reach my hand up to Jason's neck to draw him to me. The exquisite softness of his lips on mine slowly gives way to an eagerness with each surge of breath until I pull away, lightheaded with emotion, but wanting more. So much more.

"That was some kiss," Jason says nuzzling my ear, sending tingles up and down my body making me giggle. He breathes deeply, encircling me with his arms. "I've been wanting to kiss you like that since the first time I saw you."

"At the side of the road in a broken car?"

Jason shakes his head. "Charlie. I have a confession to make."

"What now?" I say releasing my hold on Jason. My hands slide from his neck to his chest where he covers them with both of his as he steps away from me.

"Well, I said that I didn't remember you from the little girl's party in the summertime." I feel Jason's heart beating fast.

"Okay."

"And I didn't want to admit to it before because..." He shakes his head and looks at the ground. "I'm an idiot."

I don't say anything but wait for Jason to explain.

"I'm an idiot, Charlie. I didn't want to admit to myself, or anyone, that I'd been so captivated by a pink fairy." He laughs then holds my hands up to his lips. "When I saw you at that party, you were so beautiful. It's hard to explain. But seeing you all sparkly with glitter and pretty wings, well, you were the opposite of a war zone. That's the only way I can tell you." Jason pulls me close. "I haven't allowed myself to feel in such a long time. It's as if I had forgotten how." He kisses the top of my head. "But then suddenly, I saw a pretty pink fairy on a hot summer's day, and..." I pull away to look up at Jason's face in the shadows. Then my fingertips touch a glistening tear on his cheek. "And there you were, again, at my gate in the storm, and my heart just melted. You got to me. You really did, Charlie." Jason presses my fingertips to his lips. He clears his throat and then continues. "I didn't want to give in to my emotions. Being detached is how I get through. We're trained to block out anything that prevents us from doing our job. In conflict, emotions make a man weak; emotions get in the way of effective decision-making; emotions blur clarity of thought. But I'm not in the military anymore. I don't need to be on high alert, always assessing risk and danger. Being here, and meeting you, I realized something. I guess I've had the time and space to think." Jason laughs. "Charlie. When you came to see me, after the storm, you showed me that I'd been carrying conflict around inside me. Now, that was something that hit hard. But I don't want to do that anymore. I don't need to do that anymore." Jason holds up his wrist displaying a digital readout. "I don't want to be that guy who only knows he's alive because an electronic device on his wrist shows a green check mark. Ha." Jason takes a deep breath. "Charlie. Can you help me? Can you help me relearn how to feel?"

"Alright," I say smiling as I stroke Jason's handsome face. "If it snows, do you think you can make a snow angel?"

"I can try."

"Well then. You don't need me to show you how to feel," I say quietly taking Jason's hand. "You're already there."

Jason is about to kiss me again when there's a noise nearby and Rocko barges his way between us to be first to go inside.

"He knows it's dinnertime," Jason says as he ruffles the big dog's ears. "Don't you, boy?" Jason entwines his fingers with mine as he opens the door to the warm and cozy tiny gatehouse.

Chapter 23

Jason

One year later

Charlie finds me in the living room putting the last bottle of chilled champagne into an ice bucket. As she reaches up to straighten my bow tie, I snake my arms around her waist and kiss her neck which makes her giggle. I love the way Charlie giggles.

"Stop. Stop. Stop," she says, pulling away and wrinkling her nose. "Guests will be arriving soon, and you'll smudge my lipstick."

"Let the lipstick be smudged," I growl kissing Charlie's neck again. "I want to kiss you." Charlie giggles some more as I squeeze her tight and breathe in her perfume. "I can't get enough of you, woman."

It's hard to believe that it's been a whole year since I showed my business partners around the dilapidated mansion. The process has been a wild and rocky ride, but the results are absolutely worth the effort. And having Charlie here by my side has made every day a fun adventure, with lots of smoochy kissing.

Charlie, Lou, Calvin, and I decided it would be wonderful to have a New Year's party, to thank all the people who have helped us get the hotel ready for guests. It has taken most of the year to get the renovations up to scratch and certificates of compliance; to meet all the criteria so we can start operating.

One of the most taxing elements of the lengthy process was writing a detailed business plan and proposal with five years of predicted figures for the bank loan I needed. So, I'm mortgaged up to my neck. And I owe friends and family for a whole lot of extra bills that weren't factored in, and I didn't see coming. But the hotel is fully booked for summer, and we are featured as the 'funky new' venue in 'Wedding Quarterly', for 'trendy hipsters in search of unpretentious shabby chic', whatever that means. Charlie assures me it's a good thing, and the publicity should help fill up the calendar for the rest of the year.

According to these figures and projections, I calculated, that I should be debt-free by my ninety-sixth birthday. That could be a little exaggerated. And if I think too much about it, I get scared and overwhelmed by what I've taken on. But it's what I'm doing now. And I'm happy. I'm with the best people who are with me one hundred percent and believe in the business as much as I do.

I look around the living room with a glowing sense of pride, then I attempt to kiss Charlie again, who looks irresistible in her sparkly vintage dress and heels. But my amorous advances are interrupted by Calvin and Lou who walk in, hand in hand, looking every inch the glamor couple from the hotel's heyday. The theme of the party is the 1930s, and guests are instructed to come as if they are starring in *The Great Gatsby*.

"I don't know who's coming," says Lou, "But honestly, I don't think I care if no one else shows up. We are going to have the best time." She links arms with Charlie.

"You look incredible," Charlie says, admiring her friend's black and white zigzag sequined dress with matching ostrich feathered headband. She's wearing elegant long black gloves, false eyelashes, and bright red lipstick.

"You don't look too bad yourself, Charlie." Lou blows a pouty kiss. "And Jason. You look quite the handsome gentleman in that tuxedo."

Instinctively I tug at my collar that seems too tight.

"Champagne anyone?" I say as a distraction.

I pour out four flutes of light golden effervescence and raise my glass in a toast. "To us. The mansion. To what we have achieved. And to our future."

"Don't say any more," says Lou dabbing a gloved finger under her lower eyelashes. "Or I'll get emotional and that will be the end of this makeup that took an age."

We sip our bubbly wine, and I admire how fragments of light from the mirror ball dance around the walls and ceiling as it spins. Colored fairy lights festoon the walls and hang loosely on the ornate picture frames. The sound system plays popular jazz tunes of the era, put together by Charlie who says that there are some dance tracks scheduled for later. The gramophone is on show, but we decided it was too fragile to use.

Couches and chairs are arranged in small groups on one side, so the middle of the floor is clear for dancing. A long sideboard, against one wall, is replete with the help-yourself buffet and loaded with platters, silverware, ice buckets, glasses, and champagne flutes.

"It looks like a great party. Just add people." Calvin nods his approval just as Meredith, Daniel, and Maddie arrive.

My sister and her family walk in with eyes wide, and mouths open in perfect 'O's, followed by Rocko who, typically, looks as if he owns the place.

Meredith hugs me and says, "Well done, Jase. What a transformation!"

Daniel shakes my hand, and Maddie says she likes my suit and that if I was in a story, I would be the prince.

"Which means that Charlie, you would be the princess. And you're going to live happily ever after together in your palace."

"Maddie. I think you're right," says Charlie smiling at me and linking her arm through mine.

"And you're wearing Great Aunt Alice's bracelet." Maddie beams.

"Yes," says Charlie holding up her wrist so the pretty bracelet catches the light. "I love it. It was my best Christmas gift ever." She smiles at me, and I feel like kissing her again.

Christmas and I are still not the best of friends, but I can handle its annoying songs and unnecessary over-the-top tat. As long as I'm with my beautiful Charlie.

"Do you think Great Aunt Alice would like the mansion now?" I ask my niece. "Do you think that she would like to be at our party?"

"Oh, yes. I think she would love to be here." Maddie pauses for a moment and looks thoughtful. "Jason." She glances to one side and then the other. Then she beckons me to bend down closer as she whispers, "If I believed in ghosts, I'd say that Great Aunt Alice is already here. And maybe she never left."

More guests arrive. They mill around in twos and threes, chatting and drinking. I meet some of Charlie's friends and family. And I introduce her to some of my buddies from the U.N. unit, who hug me and playfully slap my shoulders.

"What have you done, Major Jase? You've changed buddy." They laugh. "But in a good way."

Charlie and I smile at each other then she leads me to the dance floor.

"I think they approve," I breathe into Charlie's hair as we sway from side to side under the mirror ball.

In what seems like a very short time, the music is cut, the main lights are switched off, and Calvin captures everyone's attention by striking the side of a crystal glass with a teaspoon. Tink. Tink. Tink.

"Ladies and gentlemen. We only have a few minutes of the old year left. Please, charge your glasses in preparation for the countdown, and make your way to the terrace for the firework display."

Charlie and I dutifully file out with the guests through the patio doors and wait expectantly. The chill is refreshing after the warmth of being inside and, thankfully, the sky is clear above. There's no sign of a snowstorm. People with watches check the time as the countdown begins. Everyone joins in with ten, nine, eight... I wrap Charlie in my arms, and we hold each other tight... five, four, three...

"... Two. One. Happy New Year!" everyone chants altogether.

Around us people are yahooing, hugging, and cheering. Charlie's eyes glitter in the evening light. I cup her pretty face in my hands, then bend to kiss her lips. The champagne has made me giddy but kissing Charlie has made me see stars. We kiss as if we are alone on the terrace, under the winter night sky. We kiss as if no one else is there at all. I am intoxicated by the magic of the kiss and the wonderful night. Then, there's a crack and a pop as the firework display starts. I'm swept away on a wave of happiness. Someone close by is ooh-ing and ahh-ing as red and purple sparkles explode over our heads. A rush of gold and silver follows. Then bursts of blue rain down on the dark garden and reflect in the ornamental lake.

"Happy New Year, Jason," says Charlie. "My cheeks are sore from smiling." More ooh-ing and ahh-ing. Charlie leans her head against my chest. "I'm so pleased you rescued me."

"Oh, I think it's you who rescued me, Charlie." I kiss the top of her head. "I love you. You make me so happy." Charlie throws her arms around my neck, and we kiss again deeply, passionately, without holding back. The whole world spins in its glittering fabulous orbit into the future that I know will be filled with light and love.

The End

I hope you fell in love with Charlie and Jason. I had so much fun writing their story!

Don't miss out on the rest of the *Sweet Christmas Kisses* Series!

Scan the QR code on the next page with your phone camera then click the link.

Jingle Bells Rock and Roll by Evie Sterling
A Doctor's Snowed In Christmas Wish by Daisy Flynn
Love Rekindled at Evergreen Inn by Willa Lyons
Stuck With My Christmas Crush by Francesca Spencer
A Not So Merry Ex-Mas by Abby Greyson
A Christmas Call of Duty by Ava Wakefield
Finding Me In The Storm by Hazel Belle
Snowbound With My Grumpy Ex by Lily Waters
Sleighed By The Farmer's Daughter by Deanna Lilly
Cabin Fever With My First Flame by Madison Love
Faking It With My Bossy Ex by Leah Blair
A Holly Jolly Mix Up by Bella Greene

Don't miss the rest of the *Sweet Christmas Kisses* Series! Scan the QR code with your phone camera then click the link.

If you would like to read another one of Francesca Spencer's heartwarming tales, you can find the first two chapters of *Mr Off-limits Grump* on the next page.

What to read next

Mr Off-limits Grump

I'm stuck in a storm with a hot rock star, single dad with no memory before yesterday.

My smalltown café is my whole life.

And I am all done with happily-ever-after.

Or thought I was until Mr Grump walks in.

Scan the QR code with your phone camera then click the link.

Mr Off-limits Grump

Scan here

Start reading on the next page.

1 Jake

I'm driving but don't really know where I'm headed. I just had to drive. Leave L.A. Lah Lah Lah L.A. El Ay. I'm laughing like a crazy person. Los Angeles, the city of angels, huh? I had to put as much distance between me and that place. I don't even know why. If I was being interviewed right now and someone asked, So, what made you run off the stage and keep running, and get into your car, (at least I think it's my car) and drive and keep driving? I wouldn't be able to answer. All I know is I'm driving and I'm getting away. Far away from all that stuff. That music biz stuff. That L.A. stuff. The record company people. The publicity people. The paparazzi with the cameras; the lights; the questions. The fans.

But, no, not the fans. These are the people that gave me everything. Not them. It's the rest of it I can't deal with. I'm exhausted.

I'm a mess. My head is scrambled. I can't think. Am I having a breakdown? Do I need a shrink? Whatdoyacallit? Therapist? Everyone seems to have one these days, huh? But I don't need one because I'm a regular guy, right?

"I'm just a regular guy." That's what I say, isn't it? That is what I said, but am I?

Jeez, I think I'm having some sort of breakdown. I shouldn't have just taken off like that, without even telling Frankie. I know she'll worry. Then she'll hate me. She hates me already. I can hear her now, she's going to say something like, "Dad. This is wacko, even for you!"

The white line on the freeway is hypnotic. Each flash ticks off more distance down the road, but it's making my eyes heavy. Up ahead is a turnoff. I don't even read the name of the town, but it's ten miles away. I hope there's a gas station because the fuel light just came on.

The road winds up a hill, and even though it's dark, I see trees lining either side as I drive past. In the blackness, with my headlights showing up only a few feet of road ahead, I really have to concentrate.

After what seems like forever, streetlights appear around a corner, and, lucky for me, it's a town with a gas station. As I fill up the tank, I take a look around. Across the street, there's an old-style neon sign announcing a hotel that might just be open. I see if they have a room for tonight. It's too late to drive back home now. I need to lie down and close my eyes. This place is so quiet. All I can hear is the buzz of insects and night critters. The lack of sound is soothing like it's massaging my brain.

I'll figure things out, but tomorrow. I'm so tired. I feel like I could sleep for a thousand years.

2 Carly

"Good morning, Sheriff Sullivan. It's a beautiful day." He's in early today and he's pretty pleased with himself too, by the way he swaggered in and stands at the counter with his chest all puffed out like a pigeon.

"Good morning, Carly. Yes, it most certainly is."

I turn to the espresso machine and begin making his coffee. Like most of my regulars, I know what kind of coffee he likes - double shot large cappuccino, extra foam with chocolate.

The bright morning sun bounces off the wooden floor and tables by the window overlooking the yard. I can hear birdsong and the background rush of the river gushing through the gorge below.

I enjoy opening up. The mornings are nearly always quiet mid-week. Just the regulars stop by for their morning caffeine fixes. It's a different story at the weekend. That's when city folk come here for some R and R. It's the quiet that draws them here. And the river, of course.

I place the sheriff's cup on the counter.

"Sully. Call me Sully."

I don't say anything. I smile and nod politely. This is not the first time Sheriff Sullivan has asked me to call him by his nickname, but I would rather keep a professional distance at my place of work.

The Flow Café is not only my place of work, it is my business. It may not be generating the wealth associated with early retirement to a Caribbean Island, but it's a lifestyle choice to be here in sleepy ol' Fairwood. Yep. It's a homey little place that you probably wouldn't come to unless you were into white water rafting, or you wanted to truly get away from it all.

"There's been a report of burglaries in the area." Sheriff Sullivan pauses to sip his coffee. He then licks the foam from his top lip before continuing. Then he places his coffee cup down on the counter and hunts around in his jacket pocket. "Probably a gang, the report says. Targeting holiday places. You know, empty houses like the ones up on the ridge." The sheriff pulls out a folded printout, holding it up for me to see. It shows a blurry image of two guys walking through a glass sliding door, probably taken from CCTV footage. "If you see anyone resembling these hoodlums, just call me. I'll come right over. No problem." Sheriff Sullivan puffs out his chest again and tugs up his pants as he tucks in his shirt. "Just gotta be vigilant. Look out for each other. Be good neighbors." He says this last bit as he reaches into his pocket and pulls out some dollars, which he counts out and slides under his empty cup.

I smile like I always do with Sheriff Sullivan. It's good to stay on the right side of the local lawman, even if he thinks he's in with a chance of any kind of romance with me. Honestly, it gets a little exhausting sometimes. Sheriff Sullivan is not the only guy in town that comes into The Flow, dropping hints and flirting like a teenager at a high school prom. I have become proficient at deflecting unwanted romantic attention without losing my professionalism. But sometimes I feel like screaming, 'Go away! I have absolutely no interest in you, you strange little man in uniform, with your duck-like feet and your gut spilling over your belt and that really annoying sniff that punctuates everything you say!' No. I would never say that. I smile. I maintain politeness. I have mastered self-possession and courteous control.

"Well, thank you for letting me know, Sheriff Sullivan. I will surely keep my eyes open and let you know if I see anything suspicious."

"I know you will Carly. You are a good citizen, and I can speak for the whole town when I tell you we are glad you decided to stay, even after, you know, everything that happened." He nods at me knowingly, as if we share a secret, which we don't.

Ah yes. Sheriff Sullivan likes to remind me of the one thing I would rather forget. The fact that my fiancé, the person who brought me to Fairwood to open The Flow Café and live out our dream life in this little river community, decided to trade me in for a younger model. Literally.

Brooke, the name of the younger model, was quite simply dazzling, petite, and gorgeous with a highly effective toothpaste commercial smile. She came to Fairwood for a weekend with some gal pals and Conner, my ex-fiancé) took them on a rafting trip, then took her up on her offer of a good time.

It took me a while to recover from the initial shock of finding out the person who was supposed to be my forever mate was actually a man I didn't recognize. How could this person, Conner, who had built a business and a life and made promises to me and convinced me that he was - oh let me see if I can remember the exact words - the happiest man on the planet, just leave with someone in the blink of an eye? At the time, it didn't seem possible. It was a nightmare. He calmly told me that it was a good thing we hadn't gone through with the wedding. Imagine my family all coming over from Ireland to celebrate a sham of a relationship that was doomed to fail.

No. Conner did me a favor. I know that now. He let me keep Rusty, our dog. He was always mine anyway and liked to be in the café, while Conner was guiding on the river. He also let me have the café and all its debt. All he wanted was a quick, clean break. He wasn't going to make things messy for me. He still loved me, he said, and wanted me to be okay. And then he packed a bag, left his key on the kitchen table of our house, and left town. Just like that.

Yes. I was in shock for a long time. But then, slowly, I pulled the broken pieces of my life together. I immersed myself in running a successful business in a beautiful place. I appreciate the good things I have here. I have real friends who care for me. Jodi and Ray were angels after the breakup. They cooked for me and ran the café when I was having a gloomy day and couldn't face the world.

I don't have gloomy days anymore. I don't think about Conner anymore. Not unless someone brings him up in conversation like Sheriff Sullivan did just now. I don't know where Conner is, nor do I care. I have a great life. I really do. Now it's just Rusty and me, I am so happy. Content. Comfortable. Complete. What more could I want?

"Good morning, Carly." Jodi walks in. "And good morning, Sheriff Sullivan," she says with a broad beaming smile. She knows his romantic intentions towards me and thinks it's hilarious that he believes he stands a chance. I tell her I don't know what she's talking about and then she points out that he has never once asked her to call him Sully. "I rest my case," she says, holding up her hands like a courtroom lawyer.

Sheriff Sullivan tips his hat and leaves. More customers come in. A family with three children. A couple dressed in hiking clothes. Jodi and I are busy serving and clearing up. Then we prep for the lunchtime crowd. It's hard to predict just how many customers will come through the door. It's weather dependent, usually. When the sun's out, people feel good and will treat themselves to lunch out at a café or arrange to meet friends for a coffee and a piece of homemade cake. In summer it's pleasant to sit in the shade of the trees on the paved patio out back, where I've planted some raised beds of herbs, salads, and vegetables that I use in the café. Rusty's kennel is tucked around the corner where he likes to snooze most of the day.

The café empties out. Jodi and I chat about her husband Ray, and her kids, Lois and Jim, who are doing well at school. Café work is mostly mundane and repetitive so working with good people keeps things moving along and makes work fun. We have the stereo turned up. Jodi is making sandwiches and I'm unloading the dishwasher. We're singing away to Van Morrison when Jodi stops singing and says, "Oh my. Be still my beating heart."

Scan the QR code to keep reading
Mr Off-limits Grump.

Mr Off-limits Grump

Scan here

Thank you!

Writers need readers, so thank you so much for reading my books.

Let's keep in touch.

Visit my Amazon page or find me at

www.francescaspencerauthor.com

I have more fun romcoms coming soon, so make sure you sign up to receive reader offers and updates.

You'll get ***Mr Off-limits Grump*** to keep for free, plus a little bonus gift.

Loads of love goes out to my fabulous ARC team, my family and, of course, Chloe and Mika.

More soon.

x

Francesca Spencer

Laughs, Heart and Happily Ever After

Printed in Great Britain
by Amazon